A FATHER'S TORMENT . . .

He looked at the outline of bushes. Privacy. A hiding place. Crazy. Last place in the world that thing would be, if it had a brain, was here. And if it was just sneaking around aimlessly, chances were one in a million that it'd end up here.

It could be anywhere.

Everywhere.

It. The thing. The infant. The animal. The killer. Whatever it was, he wished they would stop calling it "his baby." They wanted to blame him. Stick him with it. It came from Lenore, for chrissake, and maybe his sperm didn't have anything to do with it. Maybe some tumor. Some weird growth.

Warner Bros.
A Warner Communications Company
presents

A Larco Production

IT'S ALIVE!

A Larry Cohen Film

Starring
JOHN RYAN
SHARON FARRELL
ANDREW DUGGAN
GUY STOCKWELL
JAMES DIXON
MICHAEL ANSARA

Music by
Bernard Herrmann

TECHNICOLOR®

**Written, Produced and Directed by
Larry Cohen**

IT'S ALIVE!

by Richard Woodley

Based on the screenplay written by Larry Cohen

BALLANTINE BOOKS • NEW YORK

Frank Davis straightened his tie and brushed off his herringbone suit and smoothed his short, sandy hair. Then he stepped from the elevator into the carpeted hallway. He nodded to the receptionist at his left, then to an assistant secretary on his right, and strode briskly into his office suite.

Once past his own secretary, in the anteroom to his office, and inside and protected from view, he slumped down into his swivel chair, rubbed his eyes, and stared at his uncluttered desk top for a few moments. Then he cleared his throat, picked up the phone, and pushed the intercom button.

"Mary, ask Buck if he can see me right now, okay? I've got some new ideas on the Marcus account that I'd like to run past him."

"I know he's got an appointment at ten, Mr. Davis."

She would have been advised of that sometime late last night. Old Buck. "Tell him I need five minutes. And coffee, black."

"Sugar?"

"No." Every day she asked, every day he said no. "Surely."

He sighed, pulled open a file drawer, and took out the manila folder marked "Marcus Toys."

His secretary rapped lightly at the door and came in, carrying a large brown mug on which was a red heart enclosing, in black letters, "Frank." She put it carefully on the desk, then stepped back primly to the door. "Mr. Clayton can see you now," she said.

She leaned back against the door, smiling, her hands behind her, her chest out.

Frank brushed by her, chuckling to himself at her pose. With the detachment of a man about to become a father for the second time, he admired her looks and enjoyed how coyly she deployed her body. Like so many of the young broads out there, she wanted to keep her job, that's all. Keep her job just long enough to find somebody to marry; then retire from all this flirtation and have babies of her own. Buck would not be the one. That's why she still posed for the field.

He walked into Buck Clayton's office without knocking, dropped the folder on the broad leather-topped desk, and sank into the soft, black-leather chair. "Whew."

Clayton turned slowly from the expanse of window overlooking Beverly Hills. "Already whew? At 9:30?" He smiled broadly as he seated himself on the edge of his desk and folded his strong arms.

Buck Clayton, the president, was a bachelor with the husky build of a football player—broader and shorter than Frank's slim 6'2"—and was dressed in a style Frank thought of as "careful casual." He wore a flowered shirt open a couple of buttons at the top, a wide white belt with a huge brass horseshoe buckle, tight white flared slacks, black Guccis. "You look tired, old man."

Frank felt like an old man, especially today, but always in the company of Clayton. Both were thirty-five, but Clayton managed somehow to make Frank feel old. Because Clayton was a bachelor and Frank a family man. And Frank always had to wear a suit and tie. Public relations was for suits and ties. Except for the president.

"I am, Buck. Lenore was up most of the night. She's really uncomfortable. She's almost due, you know."

"Yeah."

"I thought the second one would be easier."

"Yeah. Any problems with Marcus?"

"No, no, not at all. I just had a couple new ideas, looking ahead to the Christmas season, and I thought I'd better check them with you. For example, in October I thought we could plant a couple of stories about new toy safety, and set up interviews with old man Marcus himself to explain to what lengths they had gone in research and—"

Buck shook his head. "No problem, no problem. Frank, anything you want to do is fine by me. You're never wrong. You know how I feel about your judgment. Just go ahead."

"I just thought you'd—"

"Nobody in this firm is more responsible than you, Frank, or has better ideas. You're my ace. On *your* accounts, you're the boss."

"Okay. Thanks. I was also going to bring up the Sturbridge Electronics account."

"Same deal. Whatever you think. Unless there's a problem."

"No problem."

"Terrific. Nothing's wrong with Lenore, I hope."

"No, no, I guess not. The doctor says everything's fine. Just sleepless nights."

"Your son's okay?"

"Sure. Chris is fine."

"Good, good." Clayton stood up, slapped Frank on the shoulder, and went back behind his desk. "Glad everything's shipshape, Frank baby. I've got a couple guys coming in, so I better get back to work."

"Sure, right." Frank started for the door. "I'll keep you posted."

"No need. You're the perfect man for toys, right? I'll watch for the articles."

"I meant about Lenore, when the baby comes."

"Oh yeah, right."

Frank went back to his office and took out a yellow pad and began jotting down notes for the stories he would propose to the press. *New West* magazine might even go for something. They would be having a special section on toys. Or if they weren't, he would suggest it.

Yes, he was tired. Poor Lenore. Chris had been easy, but that was eleven years ago. They probably shouldn't have waited so long this time. If you could call it waiting. A truth they had never spoken about

—wouldn't even think about now—was that they hadn't wanted their first child so soon, and definitely didn't want a second on the heels of the first. So right after Chris was born came birth-control pills. For too many years. Lenore hadn't felt well when she took them, her face got splotchy. So she stopped, on doctor's advice. But they wanted two children anyway, eventually, and after a few years went by it seemed that they'd better hurry—the age difference would already be a lot. But nothing happened. Then she took fertility pills for a few months, until some magazine articles about that scared them both, and she stopped those pills too.

And six months after she stopped, she got pregnant. What wonders awaited the pill-takers! All those years and all those pills, and the result was you had one child too early, and one too—no, it wasn't too late.

And this time Lenore was a lot more uncomfortable. The whole term had been rough, but especially the last couple of months. Lenore had been scared by so many stories that she would not now take any more pills, not for anything, not even to relax and sleep. But the doctor was not worried. Everything seemed to be fine. Some people have discomforts, he said. No two children develop the same way, no mother can expect the same feelings every time. Everything was okay.

The only startling thing was that the doctor said the baby seemed to have grown unusually fast in the last couple of weeks. Any day now.

Frank spent the day roughing out the proposals for story ideas that he would suggest to various newspapers and journals. The key was to develop himself the questions they might ask, and the kinds of answers they might get—statistics, points of view, possible people to interview—stressing the importance of the subject. The key was, in fact, to do most of the work himself. The press looked fondly on stories taking minimal effort. And the main thing for the public-relations executive to do was to give them good (good = positive) ideas, accurate information, and quick accessibility to the subject.

A good public-relations man knows that the press is lazy. Everybody is lazy. That's why they take pills —the quick fix.

Frank had been able to capitalize on that fact in the campaign a year ago for Liebreich Pharmaceuticals. You couldn't say that people who took Liebreich drugs were lazy, of course. Nor did you lie. You simply stressed the positive side which every controversy has, and is easy enough to accept if you don't think too much about it.

The controversy had involved a lot of current articles suggesting that our society was too dependent upon drugs. Other drug companies ran and hid from the press. Liebreich did not. It was Frank's genius to have them volunteer for a story. The key to the press was this: Lock your door to them and they will kick it down to expose your sins; open your door and they will look for nothing, so pleased are they for easy entrée. Closed is open, open is closed.

So Frank had Liebreich open up to them, which meant the company showed them nothing, and the lambs of the press sat at the feet of the executive vice-president, nodding in friendship and respect, as he said: "I see no particular value to society in having busy, productive people waste time feeling lousy."

One of Frank's better lines. The resulting stories identified Liebreich Pharmaceuticals with candor, warmth, and concern for improvement of the human condition; while other companies, in comparison, seemed somehow related to the secretive, street-corner profiteers bent on doping our society to death.

None of this was clear in the articles, of course. Images, in public relations, are not black and white, but pleasant, suggestive fogs.

Once in a while, quite divorced from that account, Frank thought about pills. Didn't worry, just thought. Everybody lived on pills. Got through their days and nights by fooling their bodies with capsules. Frank didn't take pills. Never. If he was going to take pills, he would have done it playing guard on the basketball team at City College, when he had to play tired or hurt. Everybody on the team took them except him. Pain-killers of various types, and ups—mostly Dexes—to keep them going at full speed through four quarters of fast breaks. The center died from a liver ailment when he was thirty-three. Frank was as healthy as Jack LaLanne.

Lenore's combination of birth-control pills and fertility pills seemed like a joke. What would now be the result of such a comic mix? The result, he thought, chuckling, was that after all those contradictory tablets, you just proceeded to have a normal baby, like anybody else. Pointless. Like vitamins. You felt however you thought you felt.

Which caused him to have some impatience with Lenore. Her mother had taken twenty different vitamins and pills every day. It took him some time to convince Lenore that pills were worthless, *or* even dangerous. Early in the marriage she had taken ups for energy and downs for sleep. He got her to stop that. But then, in the after-Chris panic about family planning, she had taken up the quick-fix stuff again.

Frank's thoughts returned to his work.

"Ask Marcus if he has ever manufactured a dangerous toy." The press would love it. The good public-relations man knows that you can sell a story to the press if you seem to be on their side, suggesting a way to controversy—while you know, privately, that it can be neatly resolved to the client's benefit. And old man Marcus, well briefed by Frank, would have a splendid answer. He would welcome the question, shake his head and mutter something off-the-record about irresponsible toy manufacturers, and take the issue head-on. He would be concerned. He would give the press some pithy quotes, which Frank would compose. Something like: "My own grandchildren use my toys. I would no sooner give my granddaughter a dangerous toy than I would hand her a loaded gun."

Grandpa would sell a lot of toys.

Lenore would be a lousy public-relations person. She fretted. She worried. Most important, she made people around her nervous.

She was afraid the baby wouldn't be perfect. Who gives a goddam? If Frank were going to be a mother, he'd relax and let nature take its course. The public-relations approach would be: "Our babies are always fine, because we care, and so we take every precaution in the manufacture."

She fretted. Why does he kick so hard?

Because he's strong as an ox, like Chris.

Why is he suddenly so big?

Babies always feel big, near the end.

Why do I feel so strange, this time?

You're going to have a baby, Lenore, that's all, and the second is not the first. *We're* going to have a baby. You feel strange because you *think* you feel strange. You seem fine to me, Lenore. Why do you look at me like that?

The day passed quickly. Frank worked into the evening, and arrived home at 8:30.

For a while he sat in his tan Cadillac and looked at the house. He thought briefly about his secretary, Mary, how good she was looking to him lately, how available. But he knew why he was thinking like that: the last couple of months are always a bit rough, wife-wise.

The Marcus account had kept him late again. Lenore would wish he had been home earlier. But it was things like the Marcus account that got them this house, what they had always wanted, split-level colonial with a trim yard and a kidney-shaped swimming pool, all rimmed with thick bushes on a nice, quiet street in suburban Westwood. Good place for kids to grow up.

Of course, Lenore worked too, sometimes, substitute-teaching in kindergarten at the nearby Darwin Public School. She sure did like kids. If it had been up to her, they might have had a dozen. But they had always been in agreement, really, on spacing. Always.

The only light turned on was in the kitchen, which meant perhaps that Lenore was feeling better, and was waiting to have supper with him. A good sign.

Frank believed in signs—not omens, exactly, but signs—which he called, in his best public-relations style, indications. He acted on them. That's what first attracted him to Lenore. Something in her eyes. Strange, large, beautiful eyes. An indication. A sign nobody else would recognize. They both had it: something in their blood, as shown in their eyes, indicating, mysteriously, that they belonged together, like a species. Chris had it too, in his eyes.

Frank could swear to have seen it in her eyes again the day she became pregnant—this time. He didn't know it at the time, of course. But deep in her eyes, he recalled later, had been the announcement: at this moment she had conceived a child for them, another of their own, their blood.

This new child too would have that look in his eyes. Did he think, "his"? So big, so active, had to be a boy.

The light in the kitchen was a good indication. And so he went in cheerfully.

≫≫

Lenore lay in bed, her hands lightly on the night-gown covering her swollen belly. She didn't care what anybody said, this time she felt different. It, the baby, felt different. What nobody seemed to understand was that she didn't feel so much worried as weird. It kept her awake nights, caused her mind to wander during the days.

She was sorry it kept Frank from sleeping too. But he was just going to have to get used to the idea that having a baby was a family affair. It was not, after all, just *her* baby, but theirs—just as Chris had been. He had been angry, or at least annoyed, when she became pregnant with Chris. As if she'd done it all by herself.

When their first baby was born, Frank quite naturally loved it. "I." Or "her baby." In time, however, Chris became "*his* son," revealing quickly the same strengths and cat-like quickness of his father, with his father's eyes.

But they could as well have been her eyes. All three had the eyes of the Davis family—large, round, dark. A look some people called "intimidating" or "piercing," others described as "searching." With them, there would never be a question of parentage; their eyes gave them away. Handsome family. She combed her wavy blond hair with her fingers.

She knew he was working late on the Marcus account. That was fine. He needed to work, loved it. She did not, as he sometimes did, see public relations as a clever game. She thought it was *important*. Marcus was important, because toys were important. They had kept all of Chris's baby toys, which were good ones, and had them ready now, in the crib room, for the new arrival. Because she thought toys were so important, she had even managed to convince the school administration to stock the kindergarten at Darwin with similar toys—solid-wood toys or simple, colorful windups. No cheap metal with dangerous edges, or plastic so fragile that it cracked if you sat on it. Toys that allowed children's imaginations to roam. So successful had she been in arranging for toys that the kindergarten room resembled the room with Chris's toys here at home.

But Frank didn't think it was all that important. For boys especially. They should be strong and quick and play ball. Frank wanted a boy this time too, she knew, though he never said. A boy would be fine with her. So long as it had all its fingers and toes.

If he wanted a child at all . . . He said he did, of course. But initially they had discussed an abortion. He worried about the pills or something. But in the end they decided they really wanted the child.

And the baby would be fine. There, in the dark room, she could almost feel it talking to her, reaching for her. Almost feel its eyes on her. Davis eyes. She could almost feel it trying to dig its way out of her womb.

She felt weird.

≋

He called softly at the foot of the stairs. "Lenore?" He went up and walked into the almost-dark bedroom. He knelt next to the double bed and felt lightly around the covers. She wasn't there. "Lenore?"

He stepped into the hall and started back toward the stairs. The door to the crib room was ajar. The room was dark. He gently pushed the door open. A shape moved along the floor in the corner. He switched on the light.

"Lenore! Jesus, you scared me. What in blazes are you doing?"

"I'm sorry, Frank. I was just kind of sitting here, messing with the baby's toys."

"But why in the dark, for chrissake?"

She smiled and shook her head. "I know you'll think I'm crazy, Frank, but the baby, well, it seems to like it better in the dark. It's much calmer."

"Sure." He sighed. "You coming to bed?"

"Okay. Did you eat?"

"Baloney sandwich and a glass of milk."

"I'm sorry, I should have made you something. There's a porterhouse in the freezer for you, and—"

"I'm fine. I wasn't hungry. Drank coffee all day. Where's Chris?"

"He went to bed early, same time as me. I think

he likes to feel like I do, like he's sharing in the baby. He's very excited."

"Let's hope he stays that way, when he's got a little brother—uh, baby—to compete with."

"Of course he will, silly. He's been an only child too long. He wants the baby as much as we do. Everything's all set up with Charley?"

"He's ready any time we are. He's planning to take some time off anyway, so he's ready for Chris, any time of the day or night, for as long as we want to leave him there."

"Just while you take me to the hospital, okay? He'll want to be home with you, to get ready for me and the baby."

"Right. Let's go to bed. I'm beat."

"Go ahead. I'll be right there. Turn off the light, will you, Frank?"

Shaking his head, he turned off the light in the nursery, and went back to the bedroom. He threw off his clothes, fell into bed, and immediately went to sleep.

Lenore sat on the floor in the baby's room. "There, there, now, it's dark again. Just go to sleep, my baby." She cupped her hands under her belly and rocked slowly back and forth.

≫≫

Lenore sat up suddenly in the dark, clutching at her belly, her hair falling over her eyes. "I'm afraid," she said softly. She brushed her hair back and stared straight ahead into the night. "Frank, I'm afraid. Frank?"

Frank stirred. "Hmm?"

"I don't know why. I'm just so scared." Her voice was calm.

Frank sat up and blinked. He put his hand on her arm. "What is it? Is he kicking again?"

"More than that. It's time. The baby wants to be born."

He smiled at her, but she stared straight ahead. "D-day, hunh?" He put his hand under her hair and leaned over to give her a kiss on the cheek. "Okay. Well, we'd better get dressed."

They got out of bed. Frank switched on the light.

"Ow."

"What is it, hon?"

"The baby. The lights, I guess."

"Hey, smile, sweetheart! This is a great occasion." He took her face in his hands and kissed her firmly on the mouth.

She pulled away. "We should have packed before. We should have been ready."

"Hey, sweetheart, it'll only take a minute. We weren't ready for Chris either. He came two weeks early, remember. This character is right on schedule. That's a good trait to begin with—punctuality. Hey, what's the matter, honey?"

She stood facing the wall. "I suppose it doesn't matter how many times you've been through this before. It's still scary."

"Come on now. Not scary. Wonderful." He took a suitcase out of the closet and tossed it on the foot of the bed. "Go ahead now. You call the doctor and I'll pack."

She took the phone from the bedstand, drawing the long cord with her into the bathroom.

Frank pulled open her dresser drawers and started pawing through her clothes. "I don't know what the hell I'm looking for in this mess," he muttered. He took up armloads of clothes and dumped them into the suitcase.

Lenore came back from the bathroom and replaced the phone. "Darling, let me do that. You go wake up Chris."

"Okay, but don't lift the suitcase."

Their Siamese cat hissed from the corner. Frank reached down and picked it up. It struggled and scratched his arm. "Hey, what's got into everybody around here? Come on, Biscuit," he petted the cat to calm it, "we'll go wake up Chris." Frank hurried down the hall, his pajamas flapping around his legs.

Chris slept soundly under the model planes that hung from his ceiling. In one corner was a mound of sports equipment: football helmet and tackling dummy, two baseball gloves, roller skates, a down sleeping bag. The wall at the head of his bed was covered with posters proclaiming love and sports. On one that said, "Happiness Is a Warm Puppy," he had crossed out "Puppy" and above it scrawled in red crayon, "Baby."

For a moment Frank petted the cat and gazed down at his sleeping son, smiling. Then he lowered the cat so that it licked Chris's face.

Chris slowly turned and opened his eyes. "Hi, Dad. What time is it? Am I late for school?"

"Nope. But it's time to get up. We're going to have to drop you off at Charley's house. You can go to school from there. He's expecting you."

Chris sat up quickly. "Mom is having the baby?"

"Right. A trick she does rather well every eleven years. Now get yourself together, and don't forget your books."

Chris sprang out of bed. "Wow! Having the baby!" He sat back down. "Mom's having our baby!"

Frank tousled his son's hair and started out of the room. "Hurry up, now."

"Dad?"

"Yeah?"

"Can anything happen to her?"

"What do you mean?"

"Well, remember that movie we saw on TV, where the mother died?"

"That movie was supposed to take place a long time ago. Things like that just don't happen now. Hospitals are better, doctors are better, everybody's healthier."

"But she says the baby is so big . . ."

"Hey, come on," he laughed, suppressing his annoyance that Lenore had mentioned that to Chris. "She had *you,* didn't she? And look at the size of you, you big ox. Hurry up now, so we can get you over to Charley's."

"I'm glad I can go to Charley's," Chris smiled a little. "He's so nice to me."

"And so conveniently unattached."

"Hunh?"

"He's my best friend. He loves you almost as much as I do. Get dressed. I gotta go help your mom. She's the main one right now, you know."

"And the baby."

"And the baby. Hurry up!"

Frank got dressed, called Charley to advise him of their arrival, and started out. He stopped for a last peek in at the nursery. The white wooden crib stood in the center of the room, the colorful patchwork quilt neatly tucked in at the sides.

He grinned and chuckled. It was beautiful. Cozy. Perfect.

He carried out the two pale blue suitcases and put them in the car trunk. Then he walked back to meet Lenore coming out of the house. She was wearing a two-piece blue maternity outfit, and had a black purse slung over her arm. Chris trotted out behind her.

"You look beautiful, darling," Frank said, "just like always." He opened the car door for her, then felt his chin. "Jesus, I forgot to shave. I feel so grubby, next to you. Maybe I should just run in and—"

"No."

"Okay. Hey, hon, I was just joking. Smile a little."

"I feel so . . . I feel fine." She smiled at him.

"Can I sit in the front?" Chris asked. "So the four of us can be together?"

"Maybe on this trip you shouldn't . . ."

"That would be fine," Lenore said, standing aside

and letting Chris squirm into the middle of the seat.

The streetlights flashed by on the windshield as Frank drove. "Man, you forget how dark it is in the middle of the night."

Lenore smiled, looking straight ahead.

"You okay?"

"Fine," she answered.

"No kicking?"

"Some."

"Interesting how you women can tell just when it's time."

"The baby knows." She smiled. "The baby knows it's time."

≈≈≈

They pulled up in front of Charley's house. It was on the edge of their middle-class neighborhood, a smaller house than the others, smaller lawn, not recently mowed. Charley stood at the curb, dressed in bathrobe and slippers, the streetlight glow sparkling on his balding head. He waved to them.

"Okay, Chris, get out my side." Frank slid out and walked over to Charley. They shook hands. "Sure do appreciate this, buddy."

"Forget it, Frank. Where's Chris?"

"Right here, he's . . ."

Chris was still in the car. "Why can't I go to the hospital with you, Mom?"

"You know I'd love to have you there, but children simply aren't allowed as visitors."

"If I had my tonsils out again I could go there."

"I'll be home in three days. Or maybe sooner."

Frank appeared at the car door. "Come on, Chris."

"Maybe Charley won't like having me around."

"Charley only gets to visit his own boys two Sundays a month. And he loves kids. Come on, give your mother a kiss and let's go."

Chris leaned over and hugged his mother, holding on tight and burying his face in her neck. "Please have our baby fast."

She patted him on the head and turned him away toward his father. "We'll both call you as soon as we know if it's a brother or a sister."

He picked up his school books from his lap and slid out the door. "I don't care what it is, as long as you're okay."

"I'll be fine. Hi, Charley."

"Hi, Lenore. I'll be thinking of you. Come on, Chris, we might as well stay up, if you're game. You can help me whip together some French toast. Oh, by the way, Frank, I'm taking a week off from the store," Charley called out. "Assistant manager's going to hold the fort down and let me get in some autumn fishing. So there's no problem."

Cheerful goodbyes were waved all around, and Charley disappeared with Chris into the house.

The streetlight beat in on Lenore. She winced. "Let's get going, Frank."

〰️

The front of the small, single-level Community Hospital was bathed in floodlights. Lenore sat with her eyes closed as Frank pulled up in a no-parking zone directly in front.

He eased her out of her seat and walked with his arm around her into the nurse's station. Lenore was quickly whisked away in a wheelchair. A nurse presented Frank with a packet of forms to fill out.

"I think I did all this before," he said, scanning the papers. "When do I get to see my wife?"

"She'll be brought over to the labor room just before she's taken in for delivery, Mr. Davis."

"Is somebody taking care of her? Is everybody ready for her? Has Dr. Francis arrived yet?"

"Do you carry some form of medical insurance, Mr. Davis?"

Frank sighed, nodded, pulled out his insurance cards, and then filled in the forms.

One advantage in working for this public-relations firm was that it left no stone unturned. Everything was covered under company policies. No slipups. The name of the PR game was smoothness. No waves. No arguments. No hitches. The best PR people were invisible. So Frank was quiet, polite, efficient. He filled out the forms and took a seat nearby as directed by the nurse, though he would rather have muttered and paced. He sat placidly, while his stomach churned and he ached to cry out, "Where the hell is everybody and what the hell is everybody doing?"

Quiet. The nurses padded around on their white ripple-soles and shuffled papers. You couldn't even hear them when they talked on the phone. There was not even any medicine going-on out here. Except for their uniforms, they could have been secretaries at Clayton Associates. They never made a mistake, these nurses, because they never tried to do anything unusual. You came into the hospital, took a seat on a hard plastic chair on the shiny tile floor. And in a little while you walked out with a baby. More "medicine" went on in his own bathroom, when he shaved.

Except that he hadn't shaved. A mistake. It occurred to him that Buck wouldn't approve. A minor thing, but people noticed you when you hadn't shaved. In PR, you shouldn't be noticed. Just blend in with the background. That's why your fees were so high. People didn't know what the hell you did with their accounts, so long as you didn't screw up. And they didn't care. Most PR was a matter of keeping things quiet, smooth, unnoticeable. So businesses you represented could go on making quiet, smooth money. No questions, no arguments, no waves. But the really good PR exec, like him or Buck, took chances, caused things to happen. Caused publicity, just at the right time, in just the right way, to just the right degree. You took the chances that no out-of-control publicity would erupt. Smooth and quiet. People didn't even know why they bought Marcus toys instead of others. They were associated with goodness. Nobody knew how or why. Except Frank and Buck. Business was good, so the fees kept climbing.

Business seemed lousy at the hospital, because nobody was practicing medicine. They were, of course, somewhere in the innards of this sterile building. But Frank was being kept out of it.

And here, he was—the damn client!

In spite of himself he walked over to the nurse's station. "Look, my wife is having a baby, our baby, and I want to—"

"The nurse is here for you, Mr. Davis."

The young nurse in a pale green smock nodded to Frank and motioned for him to follow. They walked down the antiseptic corridor, Frank's shoes clacking irritatingly on the tiles a step behind the silent ripple-soles of the nurse. She directed him to a small room where she handed him a green wraparound smock similar to hers, and a gauze mask. He donned them dutifully, feeling a bit silly, then was ushered back into the corridor.

A tall, dignified man in similar green hues, with a small green cap and a gauze mask dangling loosely around his neck, came around the corner.

"Ah, Mr. Davis."

"Hello, Dr. Francis. Is everything . . ."

"Your wife will be going to delivery in a few minutes." He stuck out his hand and they shook.

"Any problems?"

He smiled mechanically. "It's going to be quite a large baby. Its growth in the last two weeks has really been amazing."

"You mean—is there any—well, is everything safe?"

The doctor smiled again and patted Frank on the back as he steered him toward a door. "The next time, Mr. Davis, you really should arrange to be present at the birth. So many men are doing it these days, and it's quite a rewarding experience. As I said, next time. It must be arranged ahead of time, so that you can be prepared for . . . for the event."

"You mean, for the blood."

He smiled again. "Yes, to be candid. It upsets some fathers. You must be ready for it. Next time."

The doctor shook Frank's hand heartily, and set off down the corridor. The nurse pushed open the swinging door and held it for Frank to pass through into the labor room.

He went quickly to the bedside of his wife, all covered in white. She was pale, her face pinched in occasional pain. She took his hand. Suddenly she closed her eyes and bared her teeth, her body tensing. She moaned softly through the contraction, then tried to smile as she looked at him.

"I'm not really very brave."

"Just keep hanging on to my hand."

She nodded. She would do that for his sake, though for her own she would have held on to her quivering belly with both hands. She couldn't truly share this time, or this pain, with him. But she knew that he felt better when she held his hand.

When she spoke, it was really to herself. "It's not like it was with Chris. It's different. I can't explain how. I couldn't make the doctor understand . . ."

"Everything's fine. I just saw Dr. Francis. Everything's fine."

Everything was fine, but different . . . strange. A strange pulse beat through her. She knew what she knew. Frank never had a baby. Dr. Francis never had a baby. Even that polite, virginal nurse never had a baby. And no one, not even she, had ever had *this* baby before.

Her body stiffened again, and she heard herself moaning. She heard—though nobody would understand that either—the baby moaning, felt it writhing for freedom. "You better call the nurse, Frank, please."

"Okay, okay. I better get Dr. Francis." He rose quickly.

"No, he'll be waiting. Just get the nurse please, Frank."

"Nurse!" Frank swung out the door and called. "Nurse! Will you please hurry up!"

The nurse and an intern scurried soundlessly into the room. The nurse looked briefly at Lenore, then exchanged a glance with the intern, who nodded.

"Sir," the intern said quietly, "you'll have to go to the fathers' room now. We'll notify you."

The fathers' room! Like some child! "Wait a minute." He bent over his wife. "I love you."

Lenore stared at the ceiling, her eyes wide. "I'm glad we decided to have this baby after all," she heard herself saying. "It wouldn't have been right to stop it. It would have been so easy and legal, but so selfish. It's right to have the baby . . ."

"Lenore sweetheart," Frank nuzzled her ear, "don't even think about that. It's going to be wonderful. We both want it."

". . . I'm going to have it after all, the baby. It won't tie you down, Frank, I'll take care of everything . . ."

Frank stared after her as the nurse wheeled her bed out and down the corridor.

He stood watching her wheeled away, until he felt the intern's impatient stare at the back of his neck. "The fathers' room. Okay?"

Three other fathers, or potential fathers, sat in the room, smoking cigarettes, staring at the floor and their knees and their hands, shaking their heads from time to time. Frank stood in the middle of the room, gazing blankly out the window into the blackness.

One of the fathers had the hiccups. Frank walked out.

He looked at his watch, lit a cigarette, and blew a

smoke ring toward the ceiling. He began walking casually up the corridor in the direction of the maternity viewing room.

"I'm sorry, sir," called a nurse dulcetly from her station, "but you'll have to go back in the fathers' room. The babies are out."

Frank looked at his watch again without noticing the time, calmly lit another cigarette, shrugged, and went back into the fathers' room.

The three other fathers were behaving as a team. Now each was filling a Styrofoam coffee cup from the glass pot on a hot plate.

"Is there anything to stir this sugar with?" asked the tallest one.

"Here, use this," said a sturdy man with a crew cut, handing the other a pencil. "I've been using it for the past three hours. After a while, you get to like the taste of lead in your coffee."

The third—a chubby, balding man who had apparently been summoned from a convocation of some sort, since he was wearing a lapel sticker that announced, "Hi! I'm Dave Bloomgarden"—stared into his steaming coffee. "I suppose you think you're joking, but there is an overabundance of lead in all the foods we eat nowadays . . ."

Frank sat down in the plastic chair opposite Bloomgarden.

". . . The fact is, we're slowly but surely poisoning ourselves, you know that?"

The other two shook their heads as they paced.

"Fine world to bring a kid into," Frank said, smiling.

"Oh, the buildup of toxic materials in our food substances is frightening," Bloomgarden went on, fixing his gaze now on Frank. "I could cite you instances of—"

"You don't have to lecture us," said the tallest man, who was dressed in a white turtleneck shirt and green slacks. "Just look out the window every day—get a load of that smog. What's the difference if we breathe it or eat it?" He did not smile.

"Maybe we'll learn to adapt to it," said the man with a crew cut. His chin was covered with stubble as was Frank's. "I'm an exterminator." He stopped pacing and looked at each of the others. "We service the Beverly Hills and Westwood area. Here's my card." He held his business card up to the tall man and Frank, then handed it to Bloomgarden, who studied it. "I'm not trying to drum up business or anything." Bloomgarden started to put the card into his jacket pocket, but the exterminator snatched it back. "The point is, years back we developed this spray to kill roaches and other household pests. But all it ended up doing was creating a new breed of roaches. Bigger and stronger and harder to kill." He nodded rapidly at his own words.

"Yeah," Frank remarked, smiling, "so maybe we'll all thrive on smog and mercury poisoning and all the rest." He looked absently at his watch. "Jesus, what's taking so long?"

The others nodded and shook their heads in chorus.

The exterminator pulled a deck of cards from the inside pocket of his plaid sports jacket. "Anybody want to join in a little game of gin?"

Nobody answered.

"I hope she's not having any trouble," Frank said softly. "She gave birth to the last one in about forty minutes. I thought they said the second one came faster."

"What are you complaining about?" said the exterminator, grinning proudly. "My wife's been in labor for six hours."

"Yeah," the other two nodded.

A baby's cry sounded down the corridor. They all turned toward the door for a silent moment, then shook their heads.

Bloomgarden stepped over to the cigarette machine in the corner and dropped coins into the slot. He waited, looking nervously around at the others, then back at the machine. He rapped it gently. Nothing came out. He slapped it. Then he pounded it, puffing mightily. "Damn thing," he whined, "stole my fifty cents!" He looked around at the others. "Stole my fifty cents, just like that." He seemed near tears.

Frank went over and took him by the shoulders, steering him away from the machine. "Here," he handed him two quarters, "here's your money back. And here's a couple cigarettes. Take it easy. Just sit down and read a magazine."

Bloomgarden sat down and shook his head.

"This everybody's first?" Frank asked. The three nodded. "My second. It doesn't help to get rattled." He smiled. The others looked grim.

The exterminator dealt a hand of solitaire. "You know what's the biggest problem in the Beverly Hills area?"

"Money," Frank said.

"Snails. Slugs and snails. They can wipe out a whole lawn in just a few weeks. The folks feel sorry for them. They're not your usual pest, not like your ants and roaches. Folks just hate seeing all them cute snails lying on their lawn dead."

Frank sighed. He walked over and leaned against the door, looking into the corridor. "Isn't anybody in a happier profession?"

"Siding," said the tall man. "Aluminum, plastic brick."

"I am," said Bloomgarden. "Mortician. My job is bringing a ray of happiness to people who are trying to cope." He smiled professionally, nodding at the others. "What's yours?"

"Public relations."

"Oh? You mean politics?"

"No, no," Frank continued, looking down the corridor, "businesses, all kinds of businesses. Toys, for example. Kids' toys."

"That's really interesting," Bloomgarden said. "Why, just think, right here in this room, we represent the care of people from cradle to—"

"Here's a magazine," Frank cut in, handing Bloomgarden a copy of *Natural History*. "Why don't you
just read for a while."

〰

In the delivery room, Dr. Francis worked between
the elevated stirrups that held Lenore's legs. Lenore
groaned occasionally, in semi-consciousness. "You're
doing fine," Francis said. "Just keep breathing evenly.
The head's on its way."

A nurse patted Lenore's brow with a towel.

"Soon, Dr. Francis?" Lenore mumbled. "Is it
soon?"

"Yes, yes. Just keep pushing, and breathing steadily.
Help me, now, if you can. Certainly is a big baby,
Mrs. Davis. Do you remember how big Chris was?"

"Seven something. Oooh, it hurts! I'm sorry."

"Seven?" Dr. Francis glanced around at the nurses
and interns assisting him. "This one will be at least
ten, maybe eleven, or more."

He stepped away from Lenore and leaned close to
the intern. "Enormous," he whispered. "Very strange."

Suddenly Lenore convulsed in a drawn-out moan.
"It wants to be *born*, doctor, can't you *see*? It wants
to be born *now!*"

Dr. Francis and the intern quickly stepped back to
their work. "Head's coming now, Mrs. Davis, right
now. There, I just cut you a little. That wasn't bad,
was it?"

Her head rocked back and forth.

"Now, the head, a little more. I'm putting the forceps on the baby's head now. Help me a little, one
more push . . ."

The intern's eyes widened, and he stumbled back
against the wall, staring . . .

⋙

Frank leaned against the fathers'-room door, staring idly down the corridor, at the far end of which he could see the double swinging doors leading to the delivery room.

A scream came from behind those doors. Then another, many. The delivery-room doors swung violently open, and a doctor staggered out. His green uniform and gauze mask were spattered with blood, and he clutched at his throat with his rubber gloves. He lurched several steps, gargling in his own blood, and fell, still clutching his throat.

To the screams from the delivery room were added those of the nurses at their station as they gaped, horrified.

Frank tore down the corridor and dropped to his knees beside the doctor. He carefully pulled down the mask, and saw that it was Dr. Francis. "What, doctor? What?" He sprang to his feet and spun wildly around, looking for help.

More piercing screams came from the delivery room, then crashes of metal and glass.

Frank was by now surrounded by nurses, standing or on their knees, quaking, crying hysterically. He pushed savagely through them, fighting his way to the delivery-room doors, unable to hear Dr. Francis choke on his last words, "It's . . . alive . . ."

"He's dying!" a nurse sobbed behind him. "The doctor's dying!"

Frank burst through the doors and down the short hallway to the delivery room itself.

And then he stopped, swayed, and groped for support against the door, staring in at a scene of carnage. He slid inside and along the wall of the room, shaking his head slowly in stunned disbelief.

Interns and nurses were sprawled grotesquely around the floor in pools of blood. Equipment tables were upended, surgical gear scattered around the room. In the middle of it, rising above the massacre on the silver steel bed sheathed in white, lay Lenore, her legs still in the stirrups. She was quiet and still.

"Lenore, Lenore—" Frank choked and stumbled toward her, coughing. He slipped in the blood and fell over her, clutching her, hugging her. "Lenore—"

Her eyes opened slowly. "My baby? My baby?"

"My god, Lenore, what happened? What happened, Lenore?"

"Where's my baby?"

An intern, propped in a corner like a torn rag doll, groaned softly. His eyes opened, then closed. He raised a hand to his ripped throat, then dropped it.

Other doctors and nurses now raced into the room, stopping short just inside the door when they met the scene. Then they began scrambling over the bodies. The intern in the corner gasped and gurgled. A doctor bent over him.

"Alive . . . gone . . ." The intern raised his eyes to the ceiling, to the skylight, then fell over on his side, his head thumping onto the floor, his eyes still staring.

The doctor bending over him looked up into the skylight. A small hole had been broken through it, the jagged edges of glass tinged with blood.

"Everyone's dead," whimpered a nurse, who sank to her hands and knees.

"Where's my baby . . ." Lenore murmured.

"WHERE'S OUR BABY?" Frank screamed. He reached out this way and that, clutching at the doctors and nurses who were slipping and falling in the gore to check the bodies for life. "WHERE THE HELL'S OUR BABY?"

Two sets of arms clamped him from the rear. He struggled insanely, but they pulled him away from Lenore and pinned him against the wall.

A doctor hunched over Lenore, examining her

quickly. He turned to Frank, his face expressionless, his voice icily calm. "Your wife's going to be all right. She's not hurt. She's all right."

"The baby—she had the baby, didn't she?"

"Yes. Of course. The umbilical cord has been severed." Then, low, to one of the interns: "But not surgically. More like it's been chewed through!" He nodded to the two interns who held Frank. "Better get him out of here."

A nurse keeled over in a faint, and an intern toppled onto her, both becoming sick on the floor.

Frank wrestled with the arms that held him to the wall. "Where's the *baby,* for chrissake! What the hell —in God's name—Jesus Christ, somebody—"

The doctor motioned toward the door. "Get him outta here, dammit!"

Frank planted his elbows against the wall and clenched his fists as he strained against the grip of the interns. "You gotta tell me—"

"You better come with us," one of them said. "I'll get you a sedative. You can lie down. Your wife's okay. Easy now—"

"TAKE YOUR HANDS OFF ME!" Frank lurched forward and yanked one intern around, sending him slithering to his knees. "YOU GOTTA TELL ME WHERE MY CHILD IS! GODDAM YOU! SOMEBODY'S GOTTA—"

A third intern grabbed his free arm and twisted it behind him. Frank snapped his head back in pain. They steered Frank out of the room. Tears rolled down Frank's face as he stumbled along with them, but no more words came. He twisted his head back to see the doctor in the delivery room staring up at the hole in the skylight.

≋

The first siren howled in the night, then another,
and another, as from different points police cars converged on the small hospital.

Frank felt numb. He was lying on a bed somewhere in the hospital. Horrifying images swept past his
closed eyes. The place was alive with strange sounds:
feet running, beds being rolled along; voices, some
calm, some crying, some pleading, some directing.
". . . Over here, officer, this one . . . Oh my god
. . . It looks like it climbed up . . . Please, nurse,
just do as I say . . . The skylight . . . I count five,
including . . . She seems okay . . . Couldn't have
been more than two minutes . . . Nobody said anything, except that intern there . . . Maybe the wife
will be able to . . . Nobody else was in here . . .
No, officer, nobody knows anything . . . Headquarters
is sending . . . No, the hole's not big enough for a
grown . . . I'm sorry, sergeant, but that's all we . . .
Yes, autopsies . . . Like claws, an animal . . . I
don't care what the press wants . . ."

Frank opened his eyes. "Press?"

A doctor stood over him, looking closely at a hypo-
dermic needle as he depressed the plunger, sending out
a tiny spurt of fluid. "This will calm you for a little
while, relax you."

"I don't *want* to relax! I want to talk to my *wife*."

"Plenty of time." He wiped Frank's arm with alco-
hol and stuck the needle in. "We all want to talk to
her. She's the only one who might be able to tell us
what happened."

"But our baby, is it dead?"

"No sir, I don't think—"

The other doctor in the room hissed.

"That's all I can say."

Frank felt the first waves of sleep advancing on him. He struggled to stay awake. "The press, I better talk to the press . . . *I* can handle them. I know just how to . . ."

≈≈≈

Lenore stared up through the fog at the two heads above her. One had a doctor's green cap on it. The other was hatless. Gray curly hair. They were not familiar.

"It hurt," she said weakly, "it hurt very much. It was coming. The head was coming. Forceps . . . the doctor said. I must have passed out." The faces stared at her, saying nothing. "Why . . . what's wrong? Can I see my baby now? Will someone bring my baby?" She tried to rise, but had no strength. "Won't somebody say something? There isn't anything wrong with it, is there? Please answer me!"

"Just be calm, Mrs. Davis. I'm Dr. Norten. This is Detective Perkins. Just tell us whatever you remember."

"Detective? Police? Why isn't Frank here? My husband. He'll tell me everything. He'll tell *you* everything. Will someone—please get my husband?" She closed her eyes and her chest shook with sobs. "Tell me—that—my baby didn't die! Please tell me it didn't die!"

"Mrs. Davis." Detective Perkins, with his sad, furrowed face, leaned over her. "We believe your baby is very much alive. We need to know what happened to cause—"

The doctor elbowed him sharply.

Lenore looked at the detective. "I don't know. Except I had my baby. Frank will know everything. Or Dr. Francis. Why isn't Dr. Francis here?"

The doctor gently pulled the detective away from

the bed, far enough so that Lenore could no longer hear them. "I'm afraid she's not going to be able to help, just now."

"But somebody's got to—"

"Lieutenant," the doctor's voice rasped impatiently, "we've got several people dead here. They are the only ones who would know what—"

"But this one's alive, doctor—the mother. And we've got another one alive, one 'something.' Out there somewhere. I can't help the dead. I've got to know what we're after."

"You're after a baby, lieutenant, a baby that might have killed five people. That's all anybody knows."

※※

Several confused and alarmed ambulatory patients milled around the night receptionist's desk. She shook her head and tried to calm them. "I'm sorry. Just our rules for tonight. No one's allowed in the maternity section. You'll have to return to your rooms."

Nurses had run up to the patients by now, and were leading them back to their rooms.

A uniformed policeman came through the doors that led into the hallway of the maternity ward and helped the nurses herd away the frightened patients. "Sorry for the noise, folks. There's been a slight accident. Nothing for you to worry about . . ."

The receptionist was on the phone. "I'm sorry, but I really don't know exactly what's going on. I have no information. . . . That's right, they don't answer my questions either. A scare of some kind. But I'm sure it's just a precaution. You know how doctors get, about staph infections or such things. . . . Later on today, or perhaps tomorrow . . ."

A set of flashing lights appeared on a car outside. This one was not police, however, but press. White lettering on the door said, "KBOP Radio-TV." A reporter with a note pad got out and pawed his way against the outcoming crowd of would-be visitors. He was followed by a cameraman lugging his machinery, and a sound man with his audio equipment slung from a shoulder strap. They were stopped at the door by the police officer.

"Sorry—"

"Just let me see Ned Schultz, okay? The hospital PR. Get Ned out here, okay?"

The officer shut the door and retreated. A few moments later a dapper man in a blue blazer, with slicked-back black hair, came to the door. "You wanted me, Buzz? You can't get in, just can't. Everything's havoc in here."

The reporter beckoned him outside, and the PR man stepped out. "Buzz, there's nothing I can say, absolutely nothing. It's a madhouse. You'll have to deal with the cops on *this* one."

The reporter stuck out his hand. "You always play ball with us, Ned. And we always stick by you."

The PR man nodded, and they shook. Schultz's hand closed over a $20 bill. He leaned forward to speak confidentially. "Look, Buzz, I'll do what I can, okay? But you got to protect me, right? Nothing gets traced back to me. I don't know what I can get for you, but I'll get something. Move your car, okay? Around the corner . . ."

〉〉〉

Led by a police officer and a nurse, Frank approached a door on which hung a red sign: "Absolutely No Visitors."

Another policeman standing outside the door nodded at them and pushed the door open.

Frank went immediately to Lenore's bedside.

Two men stepped up to him. "I'm Dr. Norten," said the man in green, "chief resident of the hospital. This is Lieutenant Perkins, a detective. She's coming out of sedation now, Mr. Davis."

Frank ignored them both and leaned over the bed. "Lenore honey, can you hear me?" She opened her eyes gradually. "Don't be afraid, sweetheart."

"Why didn't they let you come to me before?" Her voice was languid with weariness and drugs. "Did they tell you what—"

"Just rest, darling. There's been an awful mix-up. Somebody might have . . . left with our baby, and I'm holding this hospital responsible." He glanced around angrily at the two others in the room. He hadn't meant to bring up the subject like this. "But it's okay, honey, I'll get it straightened out."

"You might as well know, Mr. Davis," said Detective Perkins in a low, firm voice, "nobody took your baby. That hole in the skylight wasn't large enough for any adult to get through."

Dr. Norten gritted his teeth as he eyed the detective. "Actually, that's correct, Mr. Davis. Apparently it exited through the skylight. There's no other way out of the delivery room, except the door, and there were people out there at all times."

Frank looked from one face to the other. "What do you mean? What are you saying?"

"We're saying," Perkins explained, his face stony, "that your baby, whatever it is, got out by itself. After attacking the others."

"No . . ." Frank stared at them, shaking his head, "no, what the hell are you—"

"I've been hearing things, Frank," Lenore said slowly, "through the door. When they thought I was asleep. Crazy things. Frank . . ." Tears rolled down her cheeks. "Why would anything like this happen? Happen to us—" Sobs stopped her voice.

Frank caressed her forehead. He looked up at the doctor. He swallowed hard. "What's going on, doctor? Has everything gone crazy? Go ahead and tell us, tell us what happened."

Norten frowned. "This, uh, baby, Mr. Davis, this baby of yours, is apparently some kind of, uh, well . . ."

"Just tell us, for chrissake!"

". . . a very peculiar being, apparently. Quite singular. Small enough to be born of your wife, obviously. Yet strong enough to attack grown people, to reach the skylight . . ."

"They've been calling our baby a monster, Frank." Lenore's face reflected her own terror at the words.

"Monster?" Frank looked at Lenore, then at the doctor, then at the detective. His eyes were pinched in attempts to comprehend. "I don't see—"

"It appears that it killed five people in that room, Mr. Davis," said Detective Perkins, "tore their throats out."

"No, no . . ."

Lenore sobbed silently.

"And escaped through the skylight, on its own. Of course, that's still speculation, partly. But that's what we got so far."

"But, but, why do you call it a monster? Did anybody *see* it?"

Dr. Norten cleared his throat. " 'Monster' would not be my word, Mr. Davis. Some kind of mutant, perhaps. Nobody alive has seen it. So we're guessing, to some degree. We want to find out, just as you do, what it is."

"But, killed? It couldn't kill. Doctor, a baby couldn't kill!"

"We don't know this baby's physical and psychological makeup. We are all creatures of flesh and blood, including this offspring. That's why I must ask you and your wife to submit to certain tests, Mr. Davis."

"I won't!" Frank clenched his fists as he wept. "I refuse! I won't have anything to do with it!"

"We think," Dr. Norten went on, "that you have an

obligation to medicine, to science—to say nothing of the law—to help us determine what might have caused this, ah, mutation."

"But this, this is *insane!*" Frank bit his lips, his eyes beseeching the others in the room. "This whole night is an insane *dream!*"

"You don't think it was anything in *us,* do you, doctor?" Lenore's eyes were suddenly clear, her voice stable. "You see, we have another child. He's eleven years old and he's perfectly normal. All his fingers and toes . . ."

Frank searched her eyes, and didn't recognize them.

". . . And the two of us, you can see we're perfectly normal too. Why, we're the most normal people in town. Frank is in public relations, and I teach school part-time. We're just fine."

Dr. Norten took a step closer to her, a sheaf of papers in his hand. "You've never been exposed to radioactivity, that you knew of, Mrs. Davis? Or undergone particularly extensive X-ray treatments? Or perhaps suffered an accidental overdose of something?"

"No!" Frank stepped between the doctor and Lenore. "None of that. Nothing. Balderdash!"

"Possible genetic damage can't be ruled out, Mr. Davis," the doctor said, blinking once.

"Nothing can be ruled out at this point in time," said Detective Perkins.

"Must I stay here, Frank?" Lenore smoothed the blanket on top of her. "I'm feeling much better now. Why can't I just go home?"

"I'm sorry," Dr. Norten said, "but we can't release you just yet."

"I've gotta get my wife outta this hellhole."

Perkins expanded his chest. "I must remind you, Mr. Davis, that the hospital has the legal right to detain Mrs. Davis, under the circumstances."

"She's not a prisoner, dammit! I'm paying the bills here."

"Tut-tut, Mr. Davis." The doctor examined his

papers. "We're not worried about the bills, I'm sure. I see here you've got all the proper insurance. Oh no, it's not the bills."

"Manslaughter," Detective Perkins said stiffly, "crime scene. This whole place is a crime scene. Roped off. Nobody enters or leaves without my say-so."

Dr. Norten patted the detective on the shoulder. "I'm sure Lieutenant Perkins doesn't mean to sound harsh. Nonetheless, we have a very serious and difficult problem on our hands. May I ask you, Mrs. Davis, how long had you been taking birth-control pills before this pregnancy?"

"Several years, doctor. But I stopped taking them a couple of years ago. For a while, more recently, I took fertility pills. But I'd stopped them too, before I got pregnant."

"Oh? That's quite odd."

"Look, doctor," Frank said, "no need to get personal."

"Only in the sense that I am, after all, a physician. Now, Mrs. Davis, the files of the late Dr. Francis indicate that you inquired about an abortion eight months ago."

"Dr. Francis is dead?"

"I'm afraid, madam, he was one of those attacked. And, yes, he is."

"Doesn't everybody consider abortion nowadays?" Frank asked, surprised at his own matter-of-fact tone. "It was just a question of convenience, and then we decided we wanted the baby."

Detective Perkins harrumphed. "We all make mistakes— Uh, I apologize for that."

Frank glared at him.

"So now," Dr. Norten went on, "let me make sure I have this. First you didn't want a child, hence the birth-control pills. Correct? Ah-hah. Then you wanted a child quite badly, hence the fertility pills. Correct? Just so. Then you considered an abortion—"

"Correct, dammit!" Frank felt like spitting, but

figured he'd be arrested. "We haven't done anything most people don't do. We're perfectly normal. This is all quackery. Can't you see what we've been through?"

"I don't like it here anymore," Lenore said softly. "The walls, the smells, the sounds in the corridors, the stories, the questions, the hurts, the bright lights— the lights scared us, in the delivery room. Everything reminds me of what happened—what you say happened. I'd like to go home now. You people can call me there, or at school."

Her tone was bland, cold. Frank didn't like it. She sounded like a recording. "Doctor, my wife is . . . This hospital will be to blame for her mental state. If you force her to stay here against her will, you'll have to answer for what happens."

The doctor turned to Perkins. "May I talk to you outside, lieutenant?"

"Yeah."

They nodded at Frank, and went out the door, leaving him alone with Lenore.

"Come over here, Frank. You haven't even touched me."

He bent over her and caressed her forehead, as he had done before, when she was waking.

"That feels good. You're not afraid of me, are you, Frank?"

He forced a chuckle. "I've always been afraid of you, especially those eyes."

"Strange to think of that, that you might be afraid of me—now."

"Afraid? Nutty idea. Why should I be afraid? There must be some rational explanation for all this."

"Yes. If it matters. Explanations don't always matter. I tried to tell you, all along. How many did it kill, Frank? Four?"

"Look, honey, I don't believe any of that—"

"Was it four?"

"Five, they said. Including Dr. Francis. But those oafs don't know what they're talking about. A newborn baby couldn't—"

"Dr. Francis. He said it was a very large baby. I remember he said that. Before he saw it. When it was still inside me. You found them, didn't you? All of them. You were the first one in there, somebody said."

-"Please, Lenore." He held her hand tightly. "Don't talk about it."

"Did you see it, Frank? You can tell *me*. I won't tell anybody. Didn't you see at least a glimpse? Did it have our eyes?"

"I didn't see anything. It was gone."

"It climbed all the way up to the skylight?"

"Lenore, please, there's no need to torture yourself about—"

"Isn't that what they said, to the skylight?"

"Yes." Frank thought he saw the briefest glint of a smile on her lips, and he shuddered.

"It must be very strong for such a little thing. Frank, doesn't anybody know what it looks like?"

"No, I guess not. Not yet. Everybody who could have seen it was . . ."

"Of course not. Nobody knows yet. But soon, everybody will know, isn't that right, Frank? Everybody will know just what our baby looks like."

He shuddered again, and gripped her hand.

"You know what, Frank? I don't think it's ugly."

"Lenore, for goodness sake, stop talking about it."

"It's just different from other babies. It's afraid and doesn't want to be hurt. It's stronger than other babies, and it gets violent when it's afraid. But I don't believe it's ugly. You don't either, do you, Frank?"

"You're exhausted, honey. You don't know what you're saying. Maybe it would be better if you stayed here, just one more day."

She looked at him, narrowing her eyes. "I want to know, do you think our baby's ugly?"

"I don't know, Lenore. I guess it's in the eyes of the beholder. And I haven't seen it."

"You don't want me to come home."

"Of course I do." He rubbed her cheek. "You know I do."

"You don't want me to come home because I had an ugly baby."

"No, no, I *do,* I don't care about the baby, I—"

"You don't care about our baby?"

He shook his head rapidly. "I do, I do! I'm going around in circles." He kissed her on the cheek and turned toward the door. "I'd better go out and check on those two, the doctor and the cop. I don't trust them. Can you imagine those jerks, trying to blame us?"

"Well," Lenore murmured softly, "we are the parents."

The strange smile again flitted across her face.

"Let's not argue," Frank said. He blew her a kiss and stepped out into the corridor.

The doctor and the lieutenant stopped whispering when they saw him.

"We've decided that your wife can go home," Dr. Norten said, "tomorrow morning. Or, that is to say, later this morning."

"So you needn't bother bringing your lawyer into this," added Detective Perkins.

"Who said anything about my—"

"I'm sure you realize," the detective went on, pulling his ear, "that it's in everyone's best interest to keep this quiet for the time being. In your business, I'm sure you understand about the timing of, er, publicity. So let's just keep this between us, at least until we find out what's become of the, er, infant."

"Christ, no word yet? Strange that nobody's seen—"

"I don't see how it could survive the night," said Norten, "without nourishment or clothing."

"Yeah," said Perkins. "Like any animal, though, it's probably holed up somewhere."

"It's not an animal!" Frank snarled. "Whatever it is, you can't classify it as an animal. It's human, buster, and that's disgusting to you, isn't it? Isn't it, Dr. Norten?"

"Um, 'disgusting' isn't a word I would use."

"Kills like an animal," huffed Detective Perkins, "according to what I've seen. And when we find it, we'll have to destroy it like a crazed animal."

Frank suddenly felt beaten. "I don't care. I suppose you have to do whatever is necessary. I don't want to hear about it, or think about it, or have anything to do with it."

"Glad you feel that way," said the detective. "Makes our job easier."

"And I hope your wife understands, as well," Dr. Norten added.

"What's to understand? It's better not to think about it."

"But we *have* to think about it," the detective said, "in *our* business."

"Of course."

Dr. Norten edged toward Lenore's door. "I'll just peek in and say good night to your wife, Mr. Davis."

"I'll drive you home, Mr. Davis, if you got nothing against a prowl car."

"No thanks. I've got my car."

"Don't leave town."

"What? Of course not. I'll be home, if you need me. Or at my office."

Frank stepped into Lenore's room behind Dr. Norten.

Lenore was sitting up in bed, combing her hair. "I'm feeling better now."

Frank took her hand. "We've resolved our little conflict. I'll be picking you up around eleven this morning, to go home."

"That's fine."

He leaned over and kissed her on the cheek. "Good night, honey."

She giggled.

"What's the matter?"

"I wonder if it's a boy or a girl. That was so important to us, wasn't it? And now we may never find out. Good night, love."

≋

Frank stepped into the corridor and almost tripped over two orderlies who were mopping the floor. He grimaced in disgust, imagining what they were mopping up. He strode briskly past the receptionist and out the front door, which one of Perkins's men opened for him.

His Corfams clopped on the concrete entranceway, echoing against the building. He stopped and listened —he didn't know for what. Police cars were parked all around, the dark forms of their drivers inside. They paid him little notice; evidently Perkins had got word outside that he should be permitted to leave Community Hospital. It was quiet out here. Slowly he scanned the thick hedges that ringed the hospital. He shook his head and continued to his car, still where he'd left it, directly in front of the hospital entrance. Police cars were parked behind it. On his windshield, glistening with dew, was a parking ticket. He snatched it and ripped it up, scattering the pieces into the street.

He slid into the driver's seat and put the key into the ignition. Then he sat still, turning his head to look into the backseat. He stared at the emptiness. Then he sighed, started the motor, and drove away.

A block down the street he passed another row of thick hedges. A segment of the hedge moved. The movement followed the path of his car for a few feet, then stopped.

Frank drove nervously, stopping abruptly for red lights, bucking forward when they changed. He spun the radio dial back and forth, and finally got a news broadcast:

". . . Police still offer no explanation for the mysterious five deaths that occurred last night at Community

Hospital in Westwood. Informed sources at the hospital allege that the deaths followed the birth, only moments before, of an infant in a mutated form. KBOP has acquired exclusive information naming Mr. and Mrs. Frank Davis, of Westwood, as the parents of the infant in question. The whereabouts of the newborn child are not known—"

Frank viciously switched off the radio and slammed his fist into the dashboard. "They named us! The bastards named us! Don't they have any PR guy at that stinking hospital?"

〰️

He pulled into his driveway, his lights picking up a glint off the backyard swimming pool. Though dawn streaked the sky at the horizon, it was still quite dark. He got out of the car and stood, slowly letting his eyes fall around the lawn, the bushes, the perimeter of the house. There was no sound save that which his hard-soled shoes made on the macadam and, as he approached the house, on the manicured grass.

Climbing the four steps to his front door, he slid the key into the lock, turned it, and shoved the door open. Then he turned and looked back again at the lawn and the shrubbery. He left the front door ajar as he switched on the foyer light, two living-room lamps, and the overhead fluorescents in the kitchen. Then he went back and shut the front door, flipped the knob of the double-lock closed, and connected the security chain.

Frank had never been in this house, at dawn, alone.

He stood for a few moments in the silence of the well-lit downstairs. Then he walked stiffly into the kitchen, feeling his muscles ache with exhaustion, and pulled open the refrigerator door. Plenty of milk (you could always tell when Chris wasn't home), cold cuts, salad greens, cheeses, various leftovers. Nothing appealed. He pulled open the freezer door of the side-by-side. Piles of meat—steak, chops, roasts, hamburger. He was too tired to wait while a frozen hunk of meat cooked. He closed the door.

He wasn't really that hungry.

He crossed the living room to the den, to the bar, and poured himself two fingers of Chivas. He wasn't really thirsty, he never drank much, but he needed to relax, and sleep. He took off his shoes. Taking a sip, he leaned on the bar. Ice. Could never take it straight. He traipsed to the kitchen, grabbed some cubes from the freezer, and headed back for the den, glancing up the stairs as he passed.

When he reached the den, he halted. Slowly and quietly he put his drink down. He looked back at the stairwell. Nonsense. He padded across the living room and looked up the stairs. Foolishness. Still . . .

He went quietly up.

Upstairs he switched on the hall light. Doors to all four bedrooms were closed, as usual. Habits. Shut the doors when you leave. You too, Chris. He opened the door to Chris's bedroom and flipped up the light switch. Just as Chris had left it—bed not made. Ordinarily there was a rule. Not last night.

He went into his bedroom and turned on the light. Of course, their bed was not made either. Lenore's dresser drawers were still open. Imagine. She'd be appalled.

The guest room was spotless, tidy, sterile, as always. Necessary, in his business. Never could tell when you had to entertain a client. Couldn't tell an overnighting client to wait in the hall while you fixed up his bed. No client had ever slept in his house. But you never could tell. Never have anything messy, in your office or your home, that a client might see. "Good PR men," Buck had once said to him, "wear clean underwear."

The nursery room. He turned the knob, pushed the

door open, and reached around, before entering, to feel for the light switch.

A yowl. Something leaped from the darkness. Frank swung his arm in front of his face and stumbled backward into the hall.

The cat landed at the top of the stairs, arched its back, then sat down and licked itself.

"Biscuit! Damm it. Whew! Been locked in there all night?" He went over and picked up the Siamese, rubbing its belly, then put the cat down and went back to the nursery and turned on the light.

Everything just as they had left it, the toys Lenore had been playing with still in the middle of the floor. He knelt to pick them up, and put them neatly back in their place in the corner. The white crib with its gay quilt stood like a forlorn shrine.

Frank backed out of the room, and quietly closed the door, as if not to wake the baby.

He went back downstairs and drained his drink. Pulling off his tie, he slumped into his soft leather den chair. The phone rang. He reached over and picked up the bar extension.

"Hello?"

"Mr. Franklin Davis?"

"Who's calling?"

"This is the Los Angeles Times. This Mr. Davis? We'd like to ask you a few—"

"Davis don't live here anymore. This is the cops."

"Please don't pull that on us, Mr. Davis. We're a responsible newspaper. There is no way of avoiding this. It's an important story, no getting away from it. And we'd like to give you the opportunity to—"

Frank slammed down the receiver, breathing heavily. Then he took the receiver off the hook and laid it on the bar.

"No more calls from those cranks!"

Then he unlocked the antique desk and pulled open the top drawer; he took out a .38 revolver, checked to see that it was unloaded, then aimed it at the wall.

"Any of those nosy newsmen come around here, I'll scare the pants off 'em."

He put the gun back. No I won't, he thought. Think if it hit the papers that a gun-crazed father threatened members of the press. Think of Clayton Associates.

He sat down and stared at the wall.

In moments he felt himself dozing. He shook his head, pulled himself painfully erect, and dragged through the living room. Checking the locks on the front door, he headed for the stairs. Then he stopped, turned, and went back through the kitchen.

The hook was in place over the cellar door.

He started again for the stairs when Biscuit brushed past him languorously. Getting no attention, the cat shrugged its shoulders and continued through the kitchen to the back door. It looked back once to see if there was any final chance for petting, and, discerning none, nosed through the two-way flap at the bottom of the door and disappeared into the night.

The back door was bolted. Frank watched the flap drop shut behind the cat, covering—he blackly enjoyed taunting himself—a hole something of the size of that he had seen at the hospital, in the skylight.

He chuckled at his own morbidity, and went to bed.

≈

The light of dawn spread dark shadows from buildings along the street. A bus stopped at an intersection lined with factories which, while silent now, would hum with activity in a couple of hours. A man in a cheap tuxedo with rhinestone-studded lapels got off the bus, carrying a trombone case in one arm and a morning paper in the other.

The bus pulled away and the man put down the case and took the newspaper from under his arm, unfolding it for the front page, when he heard a faint whimpering.

He looked up. The whimpering came again.

He knitted his brows and turned his head slowly, listening. The sound came again, low, plaintive.

A baby's cry.

"What the . . . ?"

He picked up the case and began walking slowly past the darkened factory. The cry was a bit louder. The hiccuping cry of a tiny infant. He stopped at the head of a narrow alley between buildings. The cry was coming from deep in the alley.

"Who in hell would leave . . . ?"

He searched the shadows with his eyes for signs of somebody—surely somebody was in there with the baby. He could see nothing.

Putting down his case and paper, he walked tentatively into the alley, feeling his way along the building.

"Hey, baby, easy now, it's okay. Somebody leave you here in the dark all by yourself? It's okay. No wonder you're upset. We're going to take you to a nice, warm police station. Where the hell are you?"

The cry became a wail, then a shriek.

"Hey!"

The shriek was joined by his scream. He could not see what quickly clawed the life from him.

Across a nearby back lot, a house window went up. A woman's voice. "Who's out there?"

She could hear nothing more, not even the sound of something slithering or crawling away.

The window closed.

≫≫

Police Sergeant Whipple thumbed through the pile of the night's arrest records and reports. Then he pushed them aside and picked up the morning *Times*. His eye fell immediately to the headline halfway down the front page:

FIVE DIE IN HOSPITAL;
BIG INFANT SOUGHT

WESTWOOD, October 10—Police today would not, or could not, reveal any clues in the mysterious deaths last night of three doctors and two nurses at Community Hospital.

The five had reportedly been involved in the delivery, moments before, of a baby to Mrs. Franklin Davis of Westwood. The baby is listed as missing.

The five victims (names listed below) apparently died from throat wounds similar to what might be inflicted by, as one source put it, "one of those little hand rakes you use in flower boxes."

Police spokesman Det. Lt. Pinkins said that rumors that the attacks were carried out by a mutant infant were "premature."

He said that the police were not ruling out possible murder-kidnapping, or even the explosion of some warfare anti-personnel device that could have killed the adults and propelled the infant out through the skylight, leaving a small hole (see pictures, page 5).

A confidential hospital source, however, insists that the Davis infant, as yet unnamed by the parents, was in fact a huge mutant, and that it is currently the primary suspect in the attacks.

Attempts to reach Mr. Davis, a public-relations executive with Clayton Associates in Beverly Hills, have been unavailing.

Police, already under fire recently for lackluster performance, have shrouded their investigation in secrecy, except to say that a "special unit" has been formed to work on the case and to search for the missing infant.

As often pointed out by this newspaper, such "special units" in the past have had no success at all in apprehending . . .

Sergeant Whipple wadded the newspaper into a ball and threw it at the ceiling. "This rag has been out to get us for years!" he bellowed. "And who the hell is Pinkins?"

"Perkins, sir," said a patrolman nearby. "After twenty years, they still never get it right."

"Hogwash! They make it sound like we're doing nothing! We got twenty guys out all night on this one case, risking their damn lives, and they make it sound like we don't know our assignment from a hole in the ground!"

"You call me, sergeant?"

"Oh, Lieutenant Perkins. No sir. Just this story in the paper got me so upset."

"Live with it, sergeant. That's cause we can't give em any of the true facts at this point in time. We're trying to play it low key. But don't worry, we'll get this kid. We'll solve this like we solve most tough cases."

"Sir?"

"Informants. Sooner or later somebody'll spot this kid, or mutant, or whatever, and tip us off."

"I sure hope so, lieutenant. My wife is scared to death."

"Everybody's scared. Six deaths already."

"Six?"

"Yeah. Musician on his way home early this morning. Kid caught him in an alley. We think it was the kid. It's alleged to be the kid. Same wounds—throat ripped out. We're saying it was a dog. Playing it low key."

"Whew!"

"Yeah. Whatever it is, it really gets around—fast. We're trying to get some triangulation on its movements now, see what direction it's headed in."

"Any clues?"

"Nothing solid yet. We got people calling in from everywhere. They see a shadow, they call in. They hear footsteps, they call. My guess is it'll try and get out of town."

"So the thing is still alive."

"Oh it's alive, all right. It got through one night, it'll get through more. Let me look at those reports."

"This whole thing's got me damn wrought up."

"I don't blame you, sergeant. Monster baby on the loose. But we'll get it. I won't sleep until we do."

"Nobody will, sir."

≋

Frank pushed his way through a mob of shouting newsmen at the door to his office building. Photographers' flashes went off in his face.

"Mr. Davis, can you just tell us . . ."

"What's your reaction to . . ."

"How's your wife taking all this . . ."

He shoved and elbowed reporters away. "Leave me alone! I've got nothing to say!"

Building security guards kept the press back as Frank at last reached the elevator and rode up to his floor.

As he stepped out, the heads of both the receptionist and the assistant secretary turned toward him, their conversation ceased. Then quickly they looked away. He walked quickly to his office, straightening his tie as he went.

His secretary followed him into the inner office.

"Oh, good morning, Mary. I can only stay a few minutes. I have to pick up my wife at the hospital at eleven. Can you reschedule my appointments for the rest of the day?" He thumbed through his desk calendar without sitting down.

"Sir, I think Mr. Clayton wants to talk to you."

"Tomorrow. Now, about that meeting with Marcus —maybe we could make it for cocktails at 6:30 at the Hilton. I know he wants to approve the campaign by the end of the week."

"Excuse me, sir, but I think you better see Mr. Clayton now. He said it's urgent."

"Okay, okay. I'll be right in. Take care of my schedule, will you?"

"Surely."

Clayton smiled broadly as he met Frank at the door. "Come on in, Frank, good to see you." He clapped him on the back. "Come on, sit down. You look exhausted."

Frank dropped into the leather chair.

Clayton stood behind his desk. "You eaten anything, Frank?"

"No."

"Sylvia." His secretary appeared at the door. "Get Mr. Davis a couple of poached eggs on English muffins and a side of Canadian bacon. And a tall glass of fresh-squeezed O.J. That oughta do the trick for you, Frank. Can't have you collapsing on us, right?"

"Look, Buck, I can't eat anything—"

"Go ahead, Sylvia, scoot." She bowed and left. Buck leaned forward over his desk, planting his square hands on several file folders. "You can't let this get you down, Frank. It could happen to anyone. That's what they say."

"They?"

"I spoke to the hospital."

"They tell you anything?"

"Well," he smiled, "I'm very well connected over there. Vice-president of the fund-raising committee and so forth. They were very helpful. Listen, any little thing I can do for you, just . . ."

"No, nothing, thanks. We're getting Lenore out of there today. This morning, in fact."

Buck raised his eyebrows. "You think that's wise, health-wise?"

"Mary said you needed to talk to me."

"Yeah." Buck nodded thoughtfully, turned to stare out the window for a few seconds, then looked back at Frank. He folded his arms across his chest. "Look, Frank, you've got three weeks' vacation coming, and

I think it would be a good idea if you took it now."

"But Buck, I can't. The Marcus account. The Sturbridge campaign. I'm up to my ears in work. These things can't wait, you know—especially Marcus, because he wants to approve by the end of the week. Besides, the truth is I need to work, Buck. It's something to take my mind off things."

Buck smiled and waved his hand. "Hey, fella, everything's gonna be fine. We'll take care of everything for you." His gaze hardened slightly. "Frank, our business is public relations. Images. You're so good at that, you know all about it. The best. You know what goes into it, what a good position for us is, PR-wise. And right now the fact is you're too . . . well . . . controversial. Just for the time being, of course—no fault of yours. But our clients want their PR men to be, well . . ."

"Anonymous."

Buck grinned and slapped a fist into his palm. "Right! You got it. I knew you'd understand. Nobody's got a better grip on this stuff than you. So the idea is, until you become a little less of a, a celebrity—"

"You're not taking the accounts away from me? Not now, at the last minute? Hunh, Buck?"

He waved his hand. "Oh, I know how you feel, Frank baby, but you and your wife need a vacation—more than ever. Perfect time for it." He leaned across the desk and smiled. "I've got this little place near St. Thomas in the Virgin Islands—you've heard me talk about it: exquisite spot, gorgeous, nothing but sun and sand, no phone, no newspapers. I'll let you have the key. And you can stay as long as you like. How's that? Hunh?" He spread his arms, beaming.

"Whatever happened wasn't my fault," Frank said softly, eyes on the floor, his hands damp with perspiration. "It had nothing to do with me."

"Well, about that, unh . . . course not, Frank. Nobody's talking about fault around here. Nobody's to blame. That's not the name of the game in our business, right, Frank? Only results. That's all we care about. You're top-notch in results. But these things happen, Frank. You know O'Connor, down in accounting? He's got a retarded kid. Insisted on keeping him right in his own home too. And nobody thinks about that. Nobody blames him."

"We're not talking about a retarded kid, Buck, and you know it. We're talking about a monstrosity of some kind."

"Well, sure, I just meant that your baby is—"

"Not my baby, for chrissake!" Frank was suddenly on his feet, his fists clenched. "It's not my baby! And it's not a baby at all!"

"Hey, hey, calm down." Buck came around the desk and put his arm across Frank's shoulders, pushing him back down into his chair. "Maybe we'd better not talk about it right now."

"Buck, I wouldn't wish this on my worst enemy." He looked up, his eyes moist, his voice pleading. "I just don't know how to behave. Everybody saying awful things, asking nasty questions. People sticking microphones in my face, calling me up . . ."

Clayton laughed weakly. "What you need is a good public-relations firm to handle this for you."

"Yeah," Frank tried a smile, "but you know as well as I do, this matter won't be cleared away until that—whatever it is—is dead."

"Yeah." Buck went over to the window and stared out. "Frank, on your way down, why don't you take the service elevator so you won't have to face all those media jerks, okay?"

Frank numbly hoisted himself from the chair and started out. He bumped into Buck's secretary, arriving with the tray of food. Frank nodded to her and left.

She stood uneasily with the tray.

"Sylvia," Buck said, "dump that stuff. And have them clear out Frank's desk and send all his personal belongings to his home. He won't be coming back."

≈≈≈

A young woman with long, bleached-blond hair, wearing a tight green miniskirt and a waitress's apron, stepped out of her back door. She squinted into the sunset that baked the low brown hills—really little more than scrub-covered mounds—that began some fifty or sixty feet behind her house, stretched, sighed, and headed for her Mustang.

She heard a sound from the tangled mass of scrub growth on the nearest rise, and stopped. She heard it again, a low crying.

She shook her hair back and walked slowly toward the sound, climbing into the brush. As she dipped over the top of the little hill a minute later, there came a sudden howl, and dust.

A neighbor coming out of her house moments after saw only the dust cloud drifting away in the light breeze, and what looked like a single high-heeled shoe sitting alone at the top of the hill.

"Darned neighborhood kids," she muttered.

≈≈≈

Lenore sat in the front seat of the car, alongside Frank, resting her head back against a pillow. She blinked sleepily and yawned.

Frank patted her knee. "We'll be home in just a few minutes, honey."

"I feel better already, being out of that place. I'm not going to need any more of those shots, am I? I don't like being made to sleep. I'm sure I'll get along all right if they'll just let me alone."

"I've hired a nurse for you. She'll be there every day, until this—until you're back to strength."

"I don't need a nurse, I just—"

"It's best for you, believe me."

"It's just that I—I don't know about having somebody around the house, just now . . . somebody strange, staring at me."

"No, no," he smiled at her, "it won't be like that. She'll be a really good nurse, professional."

"I'm surprised anyone would *want* to come to work for us, under these circumstances."

"Dr. Norten took care of it. Underneath that stiff exterior, he's really a nice guy. He cares about you. And listen, I've got a surprise." He pulled her over gently and hugged her. *"I'm* going to be with you all the time too. I told Clayton that I'm going to have to take my three weeks' vacation now. I insisted."

"But, Frank, what about the Marcus account?"

"Buck'll just have to take care of it himself. He needs to work on accounts more. He's getting too dependent on me."

"But wasn't it important to you, to do it yourself, after all you've put into it?"

"Just another account. It's all set up now, anyway. Buck can just run with it. Probably be a stack of new accounts when I get back. Bigger ones. I've been angling for an airline. Anyway, you're more important than any of that."

"Do you think Chris knows?"

"I spoke to Charley this morning. He kept him home from school. He hasn't told him about anything, just that you're okay. But sooner or later he'll switch on the television. There's only so long you can keep all this secret from him. Charley said he'd do his best."

"I want him home right away. I want things to be normal again. Like they were before."

"Yeah."

She stared ahead, but reached up and touched his

cheek with the back of her hand. "You know, we've been drifting apart the last few years, little by little. I was hoping that the baby would bring us back . . . together. Isn't it strange that it's doing just that? Even though it's—it's—"

"People get through these things, honey." He turned into their driveway. "We'll get through it. We're finished with it. It's just a police matter now."

He stopped the car and opened his door.

She stared out the windshield, unmoving. "It was so horrible at first, all those deaths, and then just twenty-four hours later you've adjusted to the nightmare, accepted it as being real, somehow. All that happened doesn't seem real—or else, that part of it is real, and this is not, sitting here, with you, at our home. I don't know which is real, anymore."

He took her hand, which was limp. "All of it is real, sweetheart. But the bad part is over. We survived it. We both need some sleep, some rest. In a few days, we'll be back to normal."

"What about Chris?"

"Chris? Oh, he'll understand, eventually. He'll get over it too."

"No, I mean now. Aren't we going to pick him up?"

"Uh, not just yet, hon. Let's get you rested up first."

"He'll want to come home. I want him home. To have the whole family together."

"Soon, okay? Day or two. Maybe after the . . . the—"

"The police. After the police are finished."

"Yes, honey. They may be done already. Or today sometime. They'll find it."

"Our baby."

His teeth clamped together. But he spoke calmly. "Not our baby, Lenore. Don't call it that."

She looked at him, her eyes wide and dark and deep. "That's what it is, Frank. Our baby."

≈

Detective Lieutenant Perkins and two other officers stood over the body of the late musician lying on a steel table in the coroner's lab. The coroner probed at the wounds with a steel tool.

"It must have been born with quite a set of teeth," Perkins said, working his jaws around his cigar.

"And nails, lieutenant," the coroner said. "They probably extend to an inch and a half, judging from the depth of the wounds. He went after this poor man tooth and nail. Must have jaws as powerful as a cheetah."

"Full set of works, right from day one."

"I understand that a woman in the neighborhood heard a baby's cry, right about the time this happened."

"Yeah."

"It must have been hungry, kills to eat. Besides being strong. It was able to climb up the wall of the delivery room and pull itself through the skylight. I think you're going to have quite a job cornering something like that. Not to mention its size. Something that small could hide anywhere."

"Yeah. Better watch yourself. Might be right in there on one of those slabs, when you pull it out."

"What?" The coroner cringed.

"I'll be at the hospital."

≈

Perkins chewed on his black cigar as he stared up at the damaged skylight.

"No smoking in here, lieutenant."

"It ain't lit, Dr. Norten. Now, according to our

report, the thing was able to climb up the wall there and haul itself over the ceiling and crash through the skylight. But I don't figure it quite that way."

"Well, lieutenant, clearly that's how it got out of the—"

"I know it got out through the skylight. But it didn't *crawl* up there. It didn't have to."

"How then . . ."

"It jumped, doctor. Straight up."

"You're not telling me that such a little tyke could —"

"Tyke! Haw! Listen, doctor, you better get it through your head that this ain't no regular baby we're dealing with."

"I know, I know. It's just that I'm used to using certain language, you understand, in my practice. I've never dealt with a mutant before."

"The trouble is, you keep imagining this thing is some sort of regular kid with extra long fingernails or something. What we've got here is an animal. Coyote. Hyena. Baboon. Ape. Alligator. Think more along those lines. Only worse."

"But it came from human—"

"Don't matter. Leave that to the science eggheads to worry about in nineteen hundred and ninety-nine. Right now we're tracking down an animal."

"How long do you think you'll be able to get away with it, telling people these latest killings were done by a dog?"

"Five minutes, maybe ten. Dumber folks a little longer. It wasn't one of my brainier ideas, but I just wanted to do whatever I could to keep things calm."

"But the public won't like being lied to."

"Phooey. Folks forget all the lies if you come with the truth at the end—which we will. Now, about this skylight. You see, there ain't no way to really climb up there. That's number one. Number two is: the way it kills, it doesn't go climbing up folks. All the wounds have been at the throat and face. Nothing on the legs or trunk. It leaps through the air, and hits right at the throat for the quick kill. Then it doesn't stick around. It takes off right away. That's important."

"Why so, lieutenant?"

"Because, see, it helps us know what we're dealing with. Now, I think the coroner had it right, that it killed in the delivery room out of fear and panic. But he had it wrong on this second bunch."

"How so?"

"It wasn't hungry, not like he said. Oh, it might have been hungry—who the hell knows what its feeding schedule is? But that wasn't why it killed. Because it just killed and left. I didn't dispute the coroner because I just want things to stay smooth, at this point in time. And anyway, it don't matter what the coroner says. His business is dead people. What matters to me is we catch the damn thing before he gets more business. And that means it's important that *I* know why it killed."

"And do you?"

"Maybe. Still fear and panic, I would guess. Every time. I think it cries because it wants somebody to come to it. But the people that come to it cause it to panic and strike. But then I ain't no psychologist."

Dr. Norten, his hands folded primly in front of him, gazed in awe at the detective. "So what does all that mean?"

Detective Perkins rubbed his chin and chewed on his cigar. "I'm not sure, doctor. Not yet. But I know this, and I haven't told anybody until right now: it ain't trying to leave town."

"You mean—"

"Scared as it may be, it's staying right here in our own backyard. And it's gonna kill until it finds who or what it's after. Or until *we* find who or what *we're* after. Which is *it*. Let's get outta here."

They walked down the corridor. "I must say," Norten commented, "it strikes me that it shouldn't be so difficult to find this thing. I should think it would stick out like a sore thumb, wherever it is."

"That's why you're a doctor and I'm a cop. But I get your point. See, this thing can really move. One day here, next day there. But always around the area. Now, a tyke it's not. But it ain't a big rascal either. It could hide anywhere—inside, outside, up a tree, down a hole. My original hope was that it would move only at night, and sleep during the day, when we could home in on it. It seems like it's moving all the time, day or night. That makes our job tougher. But it makes it tougher for that son of a bitch too. Cause it's gonna get tired and careless. And sooner or later somebody's gonna spot it. And if that somebody is lucky, he's gonna be able to get away long enough to drop a dime and call us."

Dr. Norten shivered. "I'm sorry, lieutenant, but all this just makes my flesh crawl."

"Mine too, doctor. But on the other hand, *I* couldn't stand working in here with all these scalpels and broken bones and kidney stones floating around."

"You have an interesting way of putting things, lieutenant."

A call came over the P.A. "Telephone for Detective Perkins . . . telephone for Detective Perkins . . ."

Dr. Norten led him to a wall phone.

"Perkins here."

"Lieutenant, we just got a call from a woman who says there's a cat cornered up a tree. Says it looks like a mutant."

"Tell her it is, and to call the A.S.P.C.A."

He hung up the phone and walked with the doctor to the main entrance.

"Lieutenant, I so much wish we knew what this infant looked like."

"Don't worry, doctor. You see it, and you'll know."

Frank sat on the living-room floor, with newspapers spread all around him. In spite of his better judgment, he had been unable to resist reading everything about the case, and had bought every paper that carried a story. Oddly, there was little new information. Police were trying to pass off the latest killings as the work of a wolf-like dog.

If only it was. He would not let Lenore see any of the stories.

He cradled the telephone on his shoulder as he scanned the pages. "Hi, Chris, how you doing? . . . Yes, Mom's home. . . . I'm very busy now. I'll tell you all about everything later."

"Dad, why can't I go to school? Why can't I go out, or have any of my friends come over. And most of all, why can't I come home?"

"I can't tell you right now. But everything's going to be okay. Mom's fine. You'll just have to trust me. Do you trust me?"

"I always do, Dad, but—"

"You'll have to stay with Charley for the rest of the week. You wouldn't mind that, would you?"

"Well, I like Charley, I really do. And he's lots of fun. But I want to see Mom and the baby."

"The baby's . . . not home yet."

"Is it sick?"

"Yeah, that's right. The baby's sick and everything here is a mess. Mom needs quiet and rest. It's easier all around if you stay where you are. You don't need to go to school—isn't that what you always say? So just catch up on your reading or build some models or something."

"Will you tell Charley to let me watch TV? He says

kids watch it too much, or something. Will you tell him it's okay?"

"Let me talk to him."

"Okay."

"Hi, Frank."

"Charley, we've got a real problem, and—"

"I know. I understand. I'll see to everything. Maybe I'll take Chris fishing up at the lake for a couple days. Good idea?"

"Terrific."

"All set then. You give Lenore my love."

"Right, Charley. Listen, nobody ever had a better friend."

"That goes both ways, Frank. Talk to you in a couple days."

Frank sat back on the floor and rubbed his eyes. Lenore's nurse, wearing a white uniform, walked by, carrying a tray with two pill bottles, a pitcher of water, a glass, and a folded towel.

"Is there anything I can get you, Mr. Davis?"

"No thanks. How is she?"

"Resting nicely, as usual."

"Then does she need those pills? She says she'd rather not have them."

"I'm only following doctor's instructions, Mr. Davis. You know, you really should try some of these tranquilizers yourself. Dr. Norten said you—"

"Just take care of your patient, Nurse Gray." He quickly shook his head and rubbed his eyes. "I'm sorry. I didn't mean to snap at you. It's just that I'm better off left alone."

"I understand, Mr. Davis. You just stay right down here and relax. I'll see to your wife."

≈

Upstairs, Nurse Gray pushed the door open quietly, and, seeing that Lenore was awake, put the tray down on the bed beside her.

"How are you feeling, Mrs. Davis?"

"Fine. More pills?"

"To relax you. Dr. Norten's prescription."

"Okay, I guess." She swallowed one pill from each bottle, and drank some water.

"Would it help you to talk about anything, Mrs. Davis? Anything that happened?"

"No . . . I don't think so."

"Sometimes it helps, you know, to talk to somebody in a professional capacity."

"I don't remember much, which is just as well."

"Try, Mrs. Davis, it'll do you good. Are you sure you didn't see it? Even get one little look?"

"No, I'm sure. I told everyone, I passed out. I guess I did. I don't remember anything."

"Perhaps you're trying to freeze it out of your mind. It must have been awful. Some people say it has teeth and claws. Did you know that?"

"Why would I know that? I haven't heard anybody say that."

"Did you know that it's killed more people than just those doctors and nurses? Were you aware that it killed a musician in an alley? And a waitress behind her house? They say it was a dog, but I believe it was your child."

"No, I don't believe it." Lenore's eyes widened, her face paled. "Why are you telling me these things?"

"Oh, there's no doubt about it, in my mind. The same kind of wounds as the poor doctors and nurses suffered in your delivery room."

"I—I—" Lenore started to cry. "What do you want me to say?"

"Say anything you feel, Mrs. Davis, and cry too, that's good for you. Get it all out. Tell me everything. Take your time."

"But please, I—" She leaned toward the nurse, and in so doing put her hand on the tray, on the towel. She snapped back her hand as if burned, staring at the towel. "What have you got under there? What is that?" She ripped the towel away. A tiny tape recorder hummed with reels spinning.

Lenore sat bolt upright, trembling, pulling the covers tight around her throat. She stared in shock and confusion at the nurse. "Who are you? What are you doing here? What do you want?"

"I'm your nurse, you can tell me anything." She backed away a step.

"Who are you really working for? I want my husband—"

"Oh, I'm a registered nurse, all right," she smoothed her dress casually, "but I also do some writing now and then, on the side. Dr. Norten—" She stopped herself.

Lenore sank deep into the covers. "You're not writing about me! Frank! I want my husband!"

"I only wanted the woman's angle on this," Nurse Gray said, now showing some nervousness. "The public's entitled to know how you feel. Don't you want them to understand? It's a public service."

"Frank! FRANK!"

Lenore moved to get out of bed. Nurse Gray pushed her back, quite frightened now herself. "Will you shut up, Mrs. Davis? I was only trying to get some information. I wasn't trying to hurt you."

"F-R-A-N-K!"

Frank burst through the door.

"She's a reporter!" Lenore whimpered. "Please make her go away."

Frank looked at his wife, then at the nurse. "What the hell's going on?"

Nurse Gray took the tray and started marching stiffly toward the door.

"Recorder. Frank, she's got a tape recorder."

Frank whirled to the tray, grabbed the tape recorder, and smashed it against the wall. "Get OUT!"

Nurse Gray trotted out, terrified, stumbled her way down the stairs and out the front door.

Frank knelt beside the bed. "Lenore, Lenore, god I'm sorry! What was that all about? What was she recording?"

"She wanted to know everything. She wanted me to talk."

"But why? For who?"

"She didn't say." Lenore cried quietly.

"Lie down now, please, just try to calm down. She's gone. It's okay."

"I don't want anyone else in here," she sobbed, "no one in the house but you. And Chris. Just our family."

"Just us, sweetheart. Just relax now."

"And Chris."

"Chris has gone fishing with Charley, to the lake. He'll be back tomorrow or day after. He's fine. Then we'll all be together."

"Nobody but our family."

"Nobody. I don't understand what happened with that nurse. I can't trust anybody. You had your pills? Good. Sleep now, darling. Just go to sleep."

With Frank caressing her forehead, Lenore gradually fell asleep.

Frank went downstairs and slumped into his chair in the den. He needed to sleep too. My god, that such a thing should happen to Lenore! Like everyone was against them. She was on the ragged edge already, he feared. No one to turn to. Thank god for Charley. He wished he could go to work tomorrow. But even if he could, he wouldn't. He wouldn't leave Lenore alone all day.

They needed the three weeks, anyway. They needed to get away—would, in fact, to St. Thomas, just as soon as she was able.

≈≈≈

A bright new day. The driver stopped his white Homes Dairy truck at the curb and went around to the back and opened one of the loading doors. Bottles and cartons in crates were stacked nearly to the roof. He whistled cheerfully as he clanked through the bottles, picking one from here, one from there, and filling his hand-carrier.

Still whistling, he strode up the sidewalk toward the porch of the ranch-style house. A breeze riffled through the hedge to his left.

Except that there was no breeze.

On the porch was a row of empty bottles, a note protruding from the top of one. The milkman set down his carrier and pulled out the note and read it.

The breeze seemed to move along the hedge, toward the milk truck.

The driver nodded, folded the note, stuck it in his pocket, took out four of the eight bottles that were in his carrier, and left them on the porch. Then, resuming his whistle, he headed back toward the truck. At the sidewalk he paused to adjust a trash-can lid that was only half on. Then he stepped into his truck, started the engine, and moved off down the road.

The bottles clinked behind him as he rolled to a stop sign. There, with the truck standing still, the bottles continued to rattle.

The driver knitted his brow. He pulled on the brake, stood and turned to lean in the small door behind the driver's seat, and adjusted the position of the nearest crates. Still the bottles farther back continued their glassy tinkling. He scratched his ear. Then he leaned far in, bending over the nearest crates to reach the farther ones, standing on his tiptoes.

He froze. "My GOD!" Suddenly his feet left the floor. He had no time to scream. A gurgle came from his throat. He saw only the narrow, long, clawed fingers that flashed toward him, digging into his neck and back and hauling him through the small door.

Bottles crashed. Out of the rear door, milk trickled, then poured in a flood, washing down over the bumper; a river of fresh white milk flowed down the gutter and disappeared into a storm drain.

Fresh white milk until it mixed with red.

〰

Detective Lieutenant Perkins was quite irritated indeed by the presence of State Police Captain Sanford and his Troopers. He didn't like them butting in. Perkins and Captain Sanford and a handful of officers under the command of each stood near a wall over which was spread a huge map of the western parts of the city. Jutting from the map were five stickpins, four with tiny blue banners on them, one with red.

Captain Sanford peered at the map, and Perkins chewed a cigar and peered at him.

"Well," said the captain, "throw out the first pitch, get the ball rolling, everybody out of the trenches, let's get this show on the road. This is serious."

"We've *been* serious," Perkins drawled, "for three days now, captain." He stepped to the map. "The red pin is the hospital where the first attacks occurred. The four blue pins represent the locations of the subsequent attacks."

"Four? I understood there were only three others."

"A motorist stopped out in the canyon to fix a flat. Found him in a ditch beside the road. Few hours ago. That makes four."

The captain squinted at the map, extending a thumb and forefinger, rotating his hand and sighting over them. "There's no pattern here, no angles, no coordinates. The thing just moves around from one place to another, killing wantonly."

"Actually," piped up one of Perkins's officers, "we think it may be heading—"

Perkins held up a palm quickly, and scowled at his junior man, chomping vigorously on his cigar. Then he turned to the captain. "You didn't expect it to have some kind of master plan, did you? After all, it's only three days old."

"Three days is too much . . . too much," Sanford said somberly, shaking his head. "I guess that's why we were called in."

"I would imagine," Perkins said.

"Manpower," the captain snapped up straight, "and clout. Equipment, personnel, entrée to the governor. We got all that. That's some kid out there." He stuck out his lower lip. "Could have used this kid in Vietnam. Appetite for combat. Guerrilla warfare. Heh-heh. Now then," he rapped on the map with his knuckles, "we could just flood the whole area with Troopers, scour it from top to bottom, flush the bugger out that way."

"I'm afraid we'd end up shooting each other," Perkins said.

"Leadership and discipline would correct that. Or, we could just slip a few plainclothesmen into the area, like ordinary citizens, you know, have them leaning on lamp posts, strolling on side streets, sitting on park benches."

"I don't think we need decoys," Perkins said. "Our problem ain't that kind of problem. We just need a careful, intelligent search."

"Choppers and binoculars. Hover all over the area, keeping eyes peeled."

"Helicopters wouldn't help us much at night, which is half our problem."

"Gas, smoke, bring him out coughing like crazy, ready to quit."

"This is a heavily populated residential area, captain. Excuse me, but I'd like to suggest that we gotta just be quiet and careful and fast. We been using a tactical quick-strike mobile force, on the road round-the-clock, coordinating with foot patrols. It's just a matter of time."

"Time, time, TIME! This thing is killing people! If only I could see what this thing looks like, just once, get a peg onto it, get my hooks into it!" He jabbed his finger into Perkins's chest. "Before it gets its hooks into *you*. Heh-heh. Listen, the orders are pretty simple. Kill the goddam thing, right?"

"Right."

"No arrest, no reading the rights."

"Nope."

"That shouldn't be hard."

"Finding it is the hard part."

"We'll do 'er, we'll do 'er. Now, you say this thing —what should we call it? You got a better name? We ought to put a code on it."

" 'Thing' " is okay. We know what you mean."

"Now, you say it's larger than a baby, but smaller than an adult?"

"Judging by the hole it got out through, right."

"But stronger than either?"

"Well, it jumped straight out that hole, in my opinion."

"Christ, must have thighs like Jim Brown. And what else?"

"We figure it must have claws of some sort, from the wounds. Beyond that, we got a blank on it. Seems like it drinks milk, like from the milk truck. Cries sometimes—some people claim to have heard it, before it killed. We don't know for sure. We know it moves around, we don't know how. Like a mole, maybe. That's about it."

"Does it bleed?"

"Who knows?"

The captain snickered. "Oh, it'll bleed all right. Wait'll it gets a taste of my magnum hollow-tips."

"We just figure it's like an animal, captain. Approach

it that way. Like a very dangerous, unpredictable animal."

"Like your damn DOG!" Captain Sanford belched laughter.

"Just to keep people from panicking, captain."

"What's the difference, get chewed up by a mad mutt, or ripped apart by some two-headed dwarf? Dead's dead."

"Well, I think word has gotten around anyway that it wasn't a dog, captain. You can't fool all of the people too long."

"Let's not let politics creep into this," the captain said sternly. "Job is tough enough. Straight ahead with it. We've got to act before more innocent people die."

"Right."

"So," Sanford pulled a large note pad from his inside jacket pocket, squatted, flipped it open on the floor, and began to sketch on it, "I've got a plan. A whole bunch of tactical mobile patrols, coordinated with foot patrols, a whole bunch of telephone operators sending important messages instantly to the field. When that pint-sized terrorist shows its hand—or claw or whatever the hell it shows—we've got it!"

"One thing, captain." Perkins bit off the end of his cigar and spit it away. "It's also got a brain. Remember that. That's why it can slip around like it does. And, at a distance of a few feet, it's quicker than we are. Keep a tight rein on your men. You let one of your men drift off by himself, you're gonna lose a cop."

〰〰〰

Dr. Norten and Professor Eckstein of the U.C.L.A. Medical Center sat on the sofa in the Davis living room. Frank paced impatiently back and forth in front of them.

"Mrs. Davis seems to be progressing very nicely," Norten said. "I'm terribly sorry about that nurse. Frightful woman. Can't understand what got into her. You must be handling the nursing job very well yourself."

"Not much to do," Frank admitted. "Well then, I guess there's nothing else to talk about."

"Actually, I and Professor Eckstein here were really hoping we could discuss a related matter with you for a few minutes."

"About what?"

Professor Eckstein fidgeted with his briefcase. "You must understand, Mr. Davis, that I'm acting on behalf of the scientific community in the interests of increasing knowledge in the field of genetics."

Frank furrowed his brow. "Come on, professor, you don't have to put it to music. What is it you want?"

"I have here several forms upon which we would appreciate your signature. We are simply anticipating the complicated legalities which might intrude upon a study of this nature."

"Let me see the papers."

Eckstein handed him the documents. "I might mention that already in excess of one hundred thousand dollars has been allocated by the university for examination of this phenomenon. We have some of the leading men in the field prepared to associate in this project, and it is hoped that their research might lead to a breakthrough in the understanding of why mutations occur."

"What you want to do," Frank said, slapping down the documents on the table, "is experiment on it."

" 'Experiment' is not a word I would use," Dr. Norten put in.

"Undoubtedly it is dangerous," said Professor Eckstein, "and will—and must—be killed. It is our hope that the brain will not be damaged. My department has already sent a memo to the authorities urging them to restrain themselves from excessive violence. If it can be dispatched by a single bullet, or preferably with a gas of some kind—"

"You want me to sign away the body."

"In a nutshell. It's your right. After all, it's your child."

"It's not *my* child!"

"As you wish. It's not for me or anyone else to judge you."

"In any event," Dr. Norten said, "an autopsy would be desirable—probably required, in fact, in such a case. But I don't imagine that you'll want to have a funeral for the child. I mean, a formal burial. All of that wouldn't be good for yourself or your wife, in her current mental state . . ."

Lenore stood silently, unseen, on the stairs, listening and clutching her robe tight around her neck, her knuckles white and trembling. Tears glistened on her cheeks. She turned and disappeared upstairs.

". . . The Medical Center," Professor Eckstein went on, "is simply willing to relieve you of this depressing responsibility. Now," he held out a pen, "if you will just sign each copy, above where your name is typed . . ."

"Christ."

Norten stood and raised his index finger. "It seems that out of every tragedy, every evil, some good can come, if we can conquer our—"

"Shut up, will you, doctor?" Frank snatched the pen from the professor, sat down at the table, and began scribbling his name on the documents. "Here. I don't care. Do whatever you want."

"That's very wise of you," the professor said, "to dissociate yourself emotionally."

Frank completed the signing and looked up from the table, his eyes softened. "I suppose it will be in all the medical journals, all the history books. 'The Davis Child,' or 'The Davis Monster.' Like Frankenstein."

"I would say it is very likely that this will be

remembered," Dr. Norten said, "long after all of us are forgotten."

Frank stood and faced the wall across the table. He chuckled sadly. "You know, when I was a kid I always thought the monster was Frankenstein. Karloff, walking around with his big iron shoes, grunting. I thought he was Frankenstein. It wasn't until I was in high school and read the book that I realized that Frankenstein was the doctor who created him, not the monster itself. Somehow, the identities get all mixed up, don't they?"

"Well, perhaps, but I don't think that's really—"

"So I wonder if people will think of the monster as 'Davis.' But you're right," he turned toward the men, smiling slightly, "it doesn't matter. It won't be forgotten. Never."

Lenore came down the stairs with a sprightly step, smiling brightly, hair combed, makeup on. "Oh, hello, you two gentlemen still here? How nice."

"Actually we were just preparing to leave," Professor Eckstein said. "I believe these," he reached for the signed documents and tucked them into his briefcase, "are mine." He closed the case and patted it.

Dr. Norten put a hand on Lenore's shoulder. "I don't suppose you've been taking those pills as you're supposed to." He smiled benevolently. "You really should, you know."

Lenore smiled back and spoke softly. "Maybe it's all the pills I've taken over the years that brought this on."

"Oh, now, pshaw. You know Dr. Francis wouldn't have prescribed anything he thought harmful. Nor would I. You really shouldn't be downstairs, should you?"

"Nonsense." Lenore brushed past him and went to the picture window and pulled open the drapes. It was growing dark outside. "It's time I was back on my feet." She turned to face them, her hands clasped together over her chest. "Why don't you gentlemen stay for dinner?"

"Oh no, we couldn't have you—"

"I believe we have some nice lamb chops in the freezer," she counted off menu items on her fingers, "and mint jelly, and a fresh green salad, and I'll make a very light angel-food cake for dessert—that's Frank's favorite."

"Truly we can't stay," Dr. Norten insisted.

Lenore bustled around the room emptying ashtrays into a waste basket, straightening pillows on the sofa, adjusting lampshades. "This place is a mess," she smiled as she moved around the room, "lots to do. But I always feel better when I'm busy. Frank," she didn't bother to look at him, "be a dear and go down to the basement and get us a bottle of Beaujolais. That will be good with the chops." She beamed over at Dr. Norten. "We keep quite an extensive wine cellar. You should see it. It's one of Frank's many hobbies. He can do so many things, a many-faceted man."

"I'm sure . . ."

"I'll see you to the door," Frank said quietly to the two medical men.

Lenore continued tidying up, humming as she worked.

The three men went outside.

"Her spirits seem surprisingly high," Norten said.

Frank didn't answer.

The doctor took a deep breath and looked off across the neighborhood. "Lovely evening. Southern California is truly so delightful, so pleasant for an old man like me. Such a nice, even temperature. Rarely too cold . . ."

His voice trailed off. He averted his face.

Never too cold. Frank suspected that the doctor was thinking the same thing. Never too cold. "That's part of our problem, isn't it, doctor?"

"Beg your pardon?"

"It doesn't get cold enough at night. Not cold enough to kill a baby animal out of its den and away from its mother."

"Yes."

"Good night, gentlemen."

Frank stepped back inside and closed the door. He watched out the window as the two men walked toward their car, talking animatedly and nodding their heads.

"They couldn't stay," Lenore said matter-of-factly, moving an armchair a couple of feet away from the wall. "That's a pity."

Frank watched them drive away and remained staring out the window.

"A nice meal, that's what you need." Lenore headed for the kitchen. "I'll bet you haven't eaten in a couple of days. Lamb chops and wine, candlelight . . ."

Frank frowned. "I'll get the wine."

He went through the kitchen to the cellar door, flipped up the hook, stepped in to the top of the stairs, and without thinking shut the door behind him.

He hated these stairs. Black. You would think that somebody building a modern house like this would put a light switch right at the door. He would wire one up one day soon, he'd always told himself.

He let his eyes adjust to the darkness for a few moments, then started down the creaking wooden steps.

At the bottom of the stairs he turned to his right, into the main basement area. Dim twilight filtered in through the small window near the ceiling, just above ground level. Shadowy shapes of storage items, piled high, lined the walls: old tricycles, cartons of clothing he kept forgetting to dump in the Salvation Army bin, sporting equipment and fishing gear tangled together, boxes of books he never would read but could not bear to throw away.

He shuffled slowly toward where the bare light bulb was hanging from the ceiling. He pulled the chain. Nothing. Pulled the chain twice more. He reached up to tighten the bulb, but it was firmly screwed into the socket. Then he unscrewed it and stuck it in his shirt pocket.

The wine rack was against the far wall. Starting toward it, he brushed between some storage stacks.

From the top of one of the stacks, a small shape wavered back and forth, then dropped, smacking Frank's shoulder. He gasped, and flailed at it. It fell to the floor. Old stuffed teddy bear.

Frank stared down at it, gasping for wind, angry at his fright. He kicked it aside and proceeded to the wine rack.

Squinting closely, he searched through the dark bottles, all lying on their sides in the tall rack. He turned them in their cubbyholes to see the labels, and finally found the Beaujolais. He held it up to the light from the small window. Good wine. Damn window. The latch had long since rusted off. Another thing he had to fix. A good wind would always blow it open.

He started for the stairs, then glanced over at the outside cellar door, a big planked door canted in above the stone steps. He walked up the steps and pushed at the door.

Padlocked from the outside, just as he knew it would be.

Entering the kitchen, he dropped the hook into its eye on the cellar door behind him, put the wine bottle down on the table, and tossed the dead bulb into the wastebasket. Then he slid open the lowest drawer in the floor cabinet and rummaged through the small tools, fuses, candles, match boxes, bits of wire, rolls of scotch tape.

"Lenore?" No answer. "Lenore, we got any more light bulbs?"

He shut that drawer and pulled open each of the others in turn.

"What is it, Frank?" Lenore walked into the kitchen, wearing a long dress, her hair freshly combed.

"Damn bulb blew in the basement. I guess I gotta go get another one."

"Not now, Frank. Pick some up tomorrow. I'm fixing dinner now."

"Okay. Listen, honey." He took her by the shoulders. She smiled up at him. "Lenore, I'm sorry that those guys came over. They just wanted to talk about some stuff. You okay?"

"Of course." She cocked her head and chuckled. "Why shouldn't I be?"

"I think you gotta take it easy, for a few days."

"Oh, Frank silly, I'm not an invalid." She turned away and went to the refrigerator and began pulling out items for dinner.

"I know how tough this has been on you."

"It *was* tough. Frank. But everything's fine now. Everything's in good hands."

"I think it's bothering you more than you know, or more than you're willing to admit."

"Sssh!" She put a finger to her lips. "This is going to be very romantic. Just the two of us, by candlelight. It'll be just like—" She turned quickly away again to the refrigerator.

"Like what, honey?"

She hummed softly as she put the frozen lamb chops on a plate on the table.

"Lenore, like what?"

She stopped and bit her lip. "Normal."

"Are you . . ." He was going to say "afraid?"

"Am I what, dear?"

"Taking your medicine?"

"I don't need that anymore."

He looked at her, then turned toward the front door. "I'm going out for a few minutes, just outside, get some air."

"Fine. I'll get everything ready—surprise you, it'll be so nice."

≋

He stood on the steps and inhaled deep the sweet, warm, fall air. Lights were on in all of the houses. Streetlights cast their strange yellow cones of glow onto the sidewalks.

Everything looked totally calm, normal. Just another evening. He saw the faint shapes of the canyon hills in the distance, and in the other direction the bright lights of Los Angeles quivering in the atmosphere.

Somewhere out there, it was not normal. It was as far from normal as it could possibly be. For what skulked, somewhere, in those shadows was not completely human, though not quite an animal. What it was exactly, he didn't know. No one knew. No one alive. An army of invading troops would be more normal than the being that lurked in some protected spot, somewhere. Not here.

Or maybe here.

A State Police car turned the corner and cruised slowly past the house, five heads inside watching out all the windows, the barrels of shotguns standing upright among them.

Frank watched it glide through the block, turn, and disappear down another street.

Or maybe right here.

He went down the steps into the yard. He walked softly a few steps, then stopped, listening. A distant stereo wailed rock. Far away. Not on this block. Laughter. A neighbor's house.

He went around to the side of his house, staying a few feet from the bushes that enclosed the property on three sides like a horseshoe, giving a semblance of privacy. A breeze rippled up, stirring the bushes and fluffing Frank's hair.

A faint, low squeal.

Frank froze in his tracks, one foot still raised in mid-step.

Was it a cry of some sort?

Again he heard it.

He went over to the wall of the house. The basement window. The breeze had teased it ajar. The rusty hinges squeaked. Taking the outside handle, he pulled it shut.

He walked around to the back. Water in the swimming pool rippled. The inflated plastic seat floated in one corner. In the darkness, he was glad he knew what it was. And he was glad he knew it was the cat, sitting there just outside its backdoor flap.

He went over to the cellar door and felt the padlock. Tugged it. Secure.

Goddam it. He was just walking around scaring himself. And probably scaring Lenore too, if she heard him rustling around out here.

He looked at the outline of bushes. Privacy. A hiding place. Crazy. The last place in the world that thing would be, if it had a brain, was here. And if it was just sneaking around aimlessly, chances were one in a million that it'd end up here.

It could be anywhere. Everywhere.

It. The thing. The infant. The animal. The killer. Whatever it was, he wished they would stop calling it "his baby." They wanted to blame him. Stick him with it. It came from Lenore, for chrissake, and maybe his sperm didn't even have anything to do with it. Maybe some tumor. Some weird growth that could just as well have occurred in any woman in the world.

Something that had never happened before. Like Jesus.

He enjoyed the analogy. Not because he was sacrilegious. But because it would be a good answer to throw out at people who called it "his baby." He would say, "What about Jesus? Who was his father?"

They would say, "God."

And he would say, "Maybe this is God's too."

And they would hate him for that. They would call him a blasphemer. They would believe even more strongly that he was the father of a monster. That maybe *he* was a monster too, because he had monster blood in his veins. Monster DNA in his genes.

But it was God's. Yes. In the final analysis, it was God's work. Just like we were, and dogs and cats, everything that breathed. And didn't breathe. That's all he meant. You had to accept it as God's. Even germs were God's creatures, right?

That's all he meant.

Maybe God was trying to tell us something. About germs and microorganisms and cells. About human cells. You are what you eat. The things we are taking into our bodies are poisons. Are they not? Do we know the effects of all the garbage we eat, drink, inhale, touch, absorb through our pores?

Weren't lots of scientific experts already warning us about that?

Couldn't God be warning us too?

And besides, how could anyone of decent morality blame him, or Lenore, for what happened? He made love to his wife, that's all. He worked hard and was a good father and husband. She was a good mother and wife. They were not, all things considered, unusual.

Except that they were the parents of a monster.

No! He shook his head and sniffed back tears. They were not the parents. Lenore had had the tragic misfortune to be but a carrier of some vile organism. They couldn't be blamed. They were already suffering more than anybody.

Except perhaps for the loved ones of those who were dead. Those who were killed by the monster. Those who would yet die, if the monster wasn't killed first.

Perhaps tonight it would be killed.

He stood at the front door and breathed deeply to calm himself. He really did need a good meal, with Lenore. He wiped his eyes. Then he went in.

The food was still on the table, still wrapped, just

as it had been when he left. The wine was unopened.

"Lenore?"

He trotted through the house and up the stairs. "Lenore?"

Lenore rolled slowly over on the bed to face him. "Hi, darling. Did you eat? Sorry, but I couldn't wait up. I just suddenly got so tired and cold. Are you coming to bed soon?"

His mouth hung open. He leaned back against the wall and swallowed hard. "Yeah, sure. Let me just finish up a couple of things downstairs."

He went back to the kitchen and began putting things back into the refrigerator and freezer.

What was wrong with Lenore? Maybe he misunderstood her. Maybe she just meant that she had suddenly felt too tired to make a big meal. That was to be expected, so soon after that . . . giving birth. But her manner, her sudden cheerfulness before. Her look. Her eyes puzzled him. He didn't want to worry about her, not because he didn't care—for he cared enormously for her—but because he didn't want to face the thought that anything was seriously wrong. She needed to rest. They both did. They needed to get away to St. Thomas and lie in the sun and forget everything. Put it out of their minds. At least for a while.

He was determined to hold himself together. He couldn't let down. His family depended upon him now more than ever, and he had to maintain control of himself. Maybe when the police were finished he would go on a toot.

He didn't think he had ever felt so tired before.

And he wished the wind wouldn't keep blowing the basement window open.

≈≈≈

She had thought the feeling would leave her, after the birth. But it didn't. Lenore still felt strange.

Of course, with everything that happened being so strange, being surrounded as she was with weird events —that could cause her feeling. But not entirely. Because she felt somewhat like she had felt before—an odd sense of foreboding, unusual tides of mood and energy. She did not feel in control of herself.

It was quite normal to feel tired, of course, after giving birth. But she didn't feel tired all the time, or cold. Sometimes she had enormous energy, and her body sweated with heat. And during those times she didn't feel like herself, she felt detached in a way, not part of what was going on around her. Or inside her.

Her breasts swelled with unused baby's milk. That caused great sadness within her, and she wished the swelling would go away, the milk would go away. She didn't need the constant reminder of what her body had been primed to do, and then been denied.

Frank was holding up well, it seemed. But he was so tired. She wished he could sleep.

She wished a lot of things. She wished she had a baby. Or that she didn't have one. Sometimes she felt guilty. Chris, a normal, healthy child, was enough. She shouldn't have wanted another one.

Or she should have wanted it sooner, had it sooner. Or never had it at all.

When she thought about it, she felt sad and guilty. But sometimes she couldn't think. Time just went by. She didn't know how.

She slept. She would not remember her awful dream. If it was a dream.

≈

"Reel it in slowly now, Chris. It'll wiggle around plenty anyway, under the water."

Chris reeled in and cast again, squinting across the lake into the low sun. "Charley, will the baby look like me?"

"I don't know," Charley said, flinging his lure far out into the lake. "Why do you ask?"

"Well, your two boys don't look alike. And I was wondering if that meant the baby won't look like me. I mean, it doesn't *have* to look like me. I was just wondering if people would be able to tell that I was its brother."

"That's the kind of thing you never can predict, Chris. Nobody can ever be sure about a thing like that. For example, both your parents have light hair, while yours is black. We don't know all that much about heredity."

"What's heredity?"

"Certain things in parents that show up in their kids. Physical things like size or build or color, or personality things like temperament—you know, your moods, patience, intelligence. Sometimes kids turn out very much like their parents, sometimes they don't. When they do, we like to say it's heredity; when they don't, we don't know what it is. We aren't so sure about some things as we like to think we are."

"I'm not sure about everything."

"I know, Chris, and that's good. Kids love to learn. Adults love to think they already know. We know how to get to the moon, but we don't understand how everything works in our own bodies. Many years ago, before you were born, I guess it was when your father and I were kids, they invented the drug called penicillin. It was a super new medicine to treat all kinds of diseases. Diseases that killed people. Penicillin worked against those diseases, stopped them. We thought we had them whipped. But we didn't know that much about it. Gradually some of these diseases developed new forms of themselves—just like through heredity—much stronger forms. And then penicillin wouldn't work on them anymore. So we developed new drugs to work against the new forms of disease. I suppose in time there will be new forms of those diseases that will be too tough for the new drugs too."

"Jeez, that's scary."

"I don't mean for it to be scary, Chris. It's just that the offspring of all living things seem to change over many years. We call it evolution. It certainly isn't all scary or bad. It's just that we don't always understand it and can't always predict it. Sometimes it's like that with kids—they develop strengths or weaknesses that their parents didn't have. Did you know that people in the days of our great-grandfathers were quite a bit smaller than people are today? People are getting larger."

"Really?" Holding his fishing rod up beside him, Chris turned to look at Charley.

"Sure. I'm taller than my father was. On the other hand, he had a full head of hair all his life, while I'm getting bald. Who knows why?"

"Will I be taller than my dad?"

"Well, I don't know. He's pretty tall. You might be. Your children might be taller than you. Or stronger, or darker, or lighter, or smarter or not so smart—or anything at all. Don't forget, you're your mother's child too. Her characteristics are mixed with your father's in your body."

"Dad's taller than you."

"He sure is. He was a good basketball player."

"How did you and him get to be friends?" Chris cast, and his line snapped back and became tangled on the reel.

"Here, let me straighten that out for you. We were friends back in college. He was on the basketball team and I was a sportswriter for the school paper. We've been friends ever since those days. We've always helped each other out, especially those times when you need a friend the most." He pulled several feet of line off the reel, until it was unsnarled; then he handed it back to Chris.

"Thanks. Why didn't you keep on writing, I mean when you got out of school? Couldn't you get a job on a regular paper, for pay?"

"Somebody had to take over my father's paint store when he died."

"Did you want to?"

"Watch where you're casting now, use your wrist, look out for the branches behind you. Did I want to? I don't know. I didn't think about it. It was just the natural thing to do."

"Do you make as much money as Dad?"

"Nope. The paint business is changing just like people are. You can't always predict what business will be like in the future. For my father, it was a good business. But now everybody wants to shop at big discount stores, where paint is cheaper. So my business isn't so hot."

"Dad always buys his paint at your store."

"Well," Charley chuckled, "I guess that's part of our being friends."

"Do you wish you were still married?"

"In a way." He chuckled again. "I'd like to be with my boys more, that's for sure. That's one reason I like being with you so much. You're almost like another son to me."

"I like being with you too, Charley, except," he arced his rod far back and snapped it forward, "that I'd like to be home with Mom and Dad and the baby. Oh-oh!"

"Yeah, you got hung up on that limb, Chris my boy." Chris's lure was hooked on a low branch behind him. "Wait a second, I can reach it. I'll get it down for you."

"I can do it." Chris trotted back, crouched, and

leaped for the branch, flicking the lure free with his fingertips.

"Hey, terrific!" Charley laughed. "That's one way you're like your dad—you both can really jump!"

Christ smiled proudly and reeled the line back onto his reel. "Maybe I'll teach the baby how to play basketball."

"Maybe, Chris, maybe. Let's go out in the boat for a while. You never know where the fish will turn up these days."

※

A group of police officers sat in the small office around Detective Lieutenant Perkins.

He gnawed on his cigar. "Okay, I know what's going on. And I know what's bothering you. You'll just have to ignore what people are saying about us and do your jobs. It's tough on me too. But that's the way it is when you got a tough case."

He spat a piece of the cigar end into the wastepaper basket. "Everybody wants to put their two bits in, second-guess you, criticize you. It's the nature of our business that we can't run around giving progress reports every step of the way. So people think we're doing nothing. Until we solve the case. Then they think we're heroes. They're wrong on both ends of the deal. But that's the way folks are. They don't ever think anything's going on until it's done. Folks think pigs are just fat-slob animals until they can bite into a good pork cutlet."

The men chuckled.

"Could I ask a question, sir?" A young patrolman raised his hand. Perkins nodded. "I just wondered, why didn't you tell the State Troopers what you think the pattern of killings indicates?"

"I did."

"Well, I know you said about it being an unpredictable animal, but I mean your theory on what the thing might be after?"

Perkins worked his lips and teeth vigorously around the cigar. "In the first place, I didn't like those guys being called in. That ain't my business, of course, and what the mayor or the governor want to do we just have to live with. But they just barge in here, trampling all over everything, thinking they're smarter than anybody. I ain't saying it's not a serious case. But it ain't a question of just calling in every Tom, Dick, and Harry cop—we got plenty of bodies to do the work. It's a question," he tapped his head hard several times with his index finger, "of using your goddam brain. That's the difference between ordinary cops and good cops. Sure, you gotta beef up patrols, have special communications, all that stuff. That's easy. It's basic. We had that set up before the Troopers came in."

He paced back and forth among the officers, his cigar growing shorter as he chewed and spat.

"So, fine, they get ordered into this, we just make more patrols. Nothing wrong with that—maybe—if they don't end up shooting at us or their own damn shadows. But as far as my *theories* are concerned, that's something else. I ain't telling them because they'd either laugh at me or try and horn in on it and run it all themselves. And they aren't up to it. They don't know the area like we do, the nooks and crannies, the holes and pipes, the alleys and stairways. They'd stumble into a goddam swimming pool in somebody's backyard and drown.

"Plus, I may be wrong. And if I'm wrong, the fewer cops who know about it the better, am I right?"

The officers nodded.

Perkins chuckled. "If I'm wrong, no sense in getting everybody in a uproar over it, 'cause I don't feel like retiring just yet. And if I'm right . . . if I'm right . . ." he stared out the window, ". . . then we gotta play it cool and quiet. A small group of us are all that's gonna be in on it, so it don't get blown. Ready to move fast. 'Cause there's gonna be some shooting. And I don't want a whole mob of cops pumping lead into half of L.A."

A sudden banging on the door. "Lieutenant! Lieutenant!" More banging. "Lieutenant! They got it! The state cops got it! May I come in?"

The door swung open and a red-faced, breathless young desk officer sprang into the room waving a piece of paper. "I just monitored the call! They got it surrounded! Some Mexican's house . . ."

≋

State Troopers ringed the yard around the small house, crouched behind bushes, nervously fingering their shotguns.

Captain Sanford clutched his .357 Magnum so tightly that his entire fist was white. His eyes, like the others', were focused on a low section of shrubbery just off to the left of the front porch. Beside him hunkered a middle-aged man in overalls and a plaid shirt.

The cry came again, a low, mournful, hiccuping cry just like a regular baby.

"That's it!" the man whispered in the captain's ear. "Just like I said when I called."

"Okay," Sanford whispered to the Troopers nearest him, "move in slowly, all together, pass the word."

The circle of Troopers emerged from the bushes and started edging toward the cluster of small shrubs, their shotguns at the ready. The captain was a step ahead.

Again the cry, unmistakable, louder.

The men crept forward. They were a few yards from the spot. The crying rose to a wail.

A car screeched up to the curb. A girl's voice yelled, "What's going on? What's wrong?"

A teenage girl and boy came running from the car, their long black hair flowing behind them. "What's WRONG?"

They broke through the line of Troopers and headed for the shrubs.

"Watch it!" Captain Sanford bellowed. "Everybody down!"

The Troopers flopped into prone firing positions.

The two teenagers parted the shrubs to reveal a stroller in which a diaper-clad baby now goo-gooed happily.

"Stay away from its fingers!" yelled the captain.

The girl picked up the baby and hugged it to her chest. "But what's wrong, officers? We just left the baby for a few minutes."

Captain Sanford stood up, brushed himself off, and gingerly approached the girl.

"You can put that leg of lamb away," she said, waggling her hand at the huge pistol.

"What the hell is going on here?" the captain asked gruffly.

"I'm babysitting," she said. "My boyfriend came by and we just left the baby for a few minutes to pick up some tacos."

"But why the devil'd you put it in them damn shrubs?"

"The mother said not to leave him alone in the house. And we put him back there so he wouldn't see us leave and get upset. He likes to be out in the sun. We thought he would go to sleep like he usually does." She kissed the top of the baby's head. "We were gone just a few minutes."

Captain Sanford clicked on the safety and jammed the Magnum down in his hip holster. "Well, goddam." He turned and glared at the man in overalls. "Why'd you call us for a thing like that?"

"It was a baby's cry, just like I read about." The man blushed deeply and fumbled with the straps of his overalls. "I couldn't see nothin'. I didn't mean no harm. Better to be safe than sorry, ain't that right?"

Captain Sanford snarled and glared at the man. "But if you live next door or something, didn't you know there was a baby in this house?"

"I don't live around here. I'm a carpenter, on a job down the block. I was just walkin' by."

Three local police cars careened around the corner, slid up to and over the curb, and came to a skidding halt on the lawn behind the Troopers. The men, led by Detective Perkins, spilled out of the cars.

"What in blazes . . ." Perkins pushed through the crowd, saw the baby, then turned slowly around to Captain Sanford. "Anybody shot?"

"Naw. False alarm. This damn plumber here don't know a baby from his uncle."

Perkins looked at the man in overalls, who stared nervously at the ground.

"Sorry, I heard a cry . . ."

By now several people had come from nearby houses and were bunched on the sidewalk, watching the scene.

"Okay, okay," Perkins waved them away, "keep it moving. Family dispute. Everybody back to their knitting."

"We were here within seconds after the call," Sanford said proudly.

"I'm sure you were."

"And I can tell you this." The captain leaned to Perkins's ear confidentially. "If it'd a been that monster brat we're after, it'd a been plastered all over the wall of that house before it could say boo."

"I don't doubt that either."

"Okay, men, back in your cars! Good trial run!" The Troopers scrambled into their cars and sped away.

"Gee, officer," said the man in overalls, standing with one toe on top of the other, "did I do something really wrong?"

"No, mister," Perkins replied. "You did exactly the right thing. You might a saved a life. As it was, I think the babysitter here performed that service just in the nick of time."

She came shyly over to the lieutenant. "I can't tell you how sorry and embarrassed I am," she said, looking at the baby who gurgled merrily at her chest. "It was wrong, leaving the baby. I hope I don't lose the job."

"You deserve to."

"I know."

Perkins turned to leave.

She took a hesitant step forward. "I was just wondering . . ." she followed him to his car, ". . . whether I should have called the police about something I saw, last night."

He stopped short and turned back to her. "What did you see?"

"Well, um, nothing really. I mean, that's why I didn't call, because I couldn't really tell——"

"Tell me now."

"Well, I was walking through the parking lot of the shopping center, you know, over on Hooper Street? I had worked late at the supermarket——that's my main job——and the stores were closed, but it wasn't completely dark. And as I was walking along, I saw something move, on the other side of the fence, on the ground. You know that picket fence they have? Well I saw something move. At first I thought it was a dog, or some squirrels. But it wasn't. I mean I don't think it was. It was getting pretty dark. I thought I saw the head of something. I can't be sure. I thought it was a head. Just the back of it. Like it was looking in the direction——"

"Look, miss, just tell me exactly what you saw, even if you're not sure."

"Well, like I said, I thought it was a head. But . . ."

"But what?"

"Now please, don't laugh at me, or call me crazy or anything——because I said I just *thought* I saw it . . ."

Perkins sighed.

". . . But I swear to God, officer, the head was *very big and bald and round,* like some kind of giant human baby."

Detective Perkins bit his cigar in two. "Then what happened?"

"It was as if it suddenly saw something, in the

other direction, like over toward the school. And then
all at once a whole bunch of leaves flew up around it,
and it was gone. Please, officer," she put a hand on his
arm and looked at him pleadingly, "don't call me
crazy. I know how it sounds. That's why I didn't tell
anybody, not a soul."

"Don't tell anybody else. Maybe you saw something, maybe you didn't. Appreciate you mentioning
it to me. Let's go, men."

They got into their cars and backed off the lawn,
leaving the girl standing there cradling the baby, her
boyfriend waiting for her at the front door.

The officer behind the wheel looked over at Detective Perkins. "What do you think, lieutenant?"

"I think she saw something," Perkins said, "maybe a
balloon. But I don't think it was a balloon."

"Looks like you've been right about it, then."

"If that's a consolation to you. But this town ain't
gonna give a damn how right I've been. All anybody's
gonna care about is that we get this job done. And
we ain't done it yet. All we know is that thing's still
loose. And it's still here, most likely."

"At least now we know for sure it's got a big, bald
head."

"We don't *know* nothing. We see, we hear, we think.
Even if that girl did see something, she couldn't be
sure about that at night. And I don't care if it's got a
bowling ball for a head. She's the luckiest person in this
town that she didn't turn up this morning with her
throat missing. Next person that sees it might not be so
lucky. So next time it's seen, it better be by us."

〰〰

The hospital was quiet, clean, and orderly—approxi-
mately back to normal. Nurses bustled soundlessly
through the corridors; doctors huddled over patients;
even the delivery room was functioning efficiently.

Nobody talked about what was now referred to as "the Davis incident." But memories of it hovered in the air, and the spirit of the personnel was more somber than before.

It was perhaps to be expected—given all the furor, tensions, misunderstandings, and publicity of that tragic time—that the hospital's public-relations man, Ned Schultz, resigned, in the best interests of everybody concerned. He was congratulated all around for his unselfishness and grace under pressure, and given a cake. He managed to find a job with KBOP Radio-TV. Dr. Norten, the chief resident, had weathered the storm. It was not, after all, any of the hospital's fault. Some felt that he, like Schultz, perhaps should resign, only because the public tended to associate him with the awful events.

But, as a direct result of those same events, the hospital was short of doctors. And Norten had, by reason of his quietly professional demeanor, been able to convince the hospital board that he above all others should be relied upon to use his experience at the hospital to keep it functioning medically well. That he should run everything, in fact.

And that he did. He was superbly organized himself, and able to transmit that skill upon his staff. So well-ordered was he that not only was he able to continue and expand his practice with patients, but also he found time to stay abreast of all details relating to the horrible occurrence of a few days before.

As a matter of fact, at his recent overnight private meeting with a publisher in Chicago, he'd been assured of a six-figure amount whenever he would be able to deliver a suitable manuscript, which he had tentatively entitled: "The Davis Incident."

"Telephone for Dr. Norten," announced the P.A., ". . . telephone for Dr. Norten . . ."

He broke off a conversation with some interns in the corridor, and took the call in his office.

"Dr. Norten? Professor Eckstein speaking. I promised I'd keep you posted. I've been going over some reports in the coroner's office. Fascinating details. But I guess you're pretty familiar with all that."

"Yes, I think so."

"But there is something I find rather curious."

"Oh?"

"Yes, in the blood samples. In the umbilical cord. Tell me, doctor, is Mrs. Davis an unusually energetic or nervous person?"

"Nervous perhaps, according to Dr. Francis's files. She seemed to have an odd feeling while she was carrying the . . . child. She was apparently not terribly lucid or articulate about it, but she used the words 'strange' and 'weird' often, according to the notes. I do remember, now that you mention it, the nurse who tended her in the labor room saying that Mrs. Davis did appear, as she put it, 'highly agitated' before she went to delivery. That is, before her husband visited her in labor. The nurse recounted to me that she seemed quite upset indeed, apprehensive not about labor pains and the usual things, but about something she didn't seem to express readily. And again, after she left her husband, when she was being wheeled in to delivery, there was something she said about it being 'too late,' and Mrs. Davis sat up. Almost as quickly, she collapsed back down on the bed, and remained relatively calm after that. Does any of this relate to what you're curious about?"

"Perhaps, Dr. Norten. And now, is Mrs. Davis feeling especially tired, more spent than you would expect?"

"Hmm. Odd. When last I saw her, yesterday, she was in fact surprisingly energetic, I thought. Surprisingly. I urged her to take a Valium and stay off her feet, but she was fairly dancing around the room.

"For how long?"

"We left within minutes, so I can't say."

"You don't know if that energy abruptly left her soon after that?"

"No. Come, come, my good man, you must tell me what's on your mind."

"Just this, doctor. In the umbilical cord, I discovered that there was an amazing supply of hormones, primarily adrenaline. The umbilical was saturated with it. It is as if every ounce of adrenaline in her body was suddenly thrust into the child. Anything in Dr. Francis's files about her hormone balance?"

"Nothing I can recall, professor."

"Had she ever been on the pill, if I may ask?"

"Why yes, in fact, for many years. Remarkably enough, she stopped taking them some time ago, then began taking fertility pills of some sort—I don't remember the make and model. Quaint ambivalence about the procreative processes, what?"

"Lord! Didn't anybody warn her about playing with her hormonal balance so flagrantly?"

"I daresay, professor, just between you and me, had she been my patient I most certainly would have counseled a more careful approach. Have you some conclusions from all this?"

"I fear I might bore you, doctor, with matters you have already contemplated."

"Tut, tut, Professor Eckstein. If I have considered what you are about to tell me, you will either confirm my conjectures or deny them. Either way, we advance our knowledge of the science and the case."

"Very well. We have here a woman who, at least at the moment of birth, infused her infant with a horrendous dose of adrenaline and other hormones. Not only would that deplete her, but it would also tend to oversupply the infant. It would be enough to kill an ordinary newborn child. But this one accepted the hormones. Such a capability would suggest grotesque consequences: abnormal growth and strength, and God knows what other abnormalities and deformities. It could even suggest why such an infant could survive in cold and damp."

"Ahh."

"But of course we must ask ourselves: How could such an infant accept this hormonal overdose at the last moment?"

"Exactly."

"Supposing we postulate that the woman was producing and transferring gross amounts of these hormones, including adrenaline, from the moment of conception and through the entire term."

"Precisely."

"It challenges standard doctrine, but were that possible, we might have found the important clue in the mystery of how this mutant developed."

"Certainly."

"And we shall know what form it finally took soon, when we have the corpus for examination."

"Assuredly."

"But *not,* doctor, precisely *why.*"

"Hunh?"

"If this theory is correct, and if our interests involve more than just the lurid, sensational, short-sighted details of the mutant itself—such as what one might find in the *Guinness Book of Records*—then we must address the riddle of why Mrs. Davis produced these massive amounts of hormones, what in her body caused them to be loosed by the truckload so as to produce this gargoyle of a child . . ."

"I should say so."

". . . Because, doctor, as I'm sure you already know, her glands may still be so afflicted, still producing in outrageous spasms."

"Quite right."

"And if they are, doctor, we must assume one of two things."

"One or the other."

"Either she is unique, in a way herself a mutant . . ."

"Or . . ."

". . . or she is not unique. If the former applies, we have a simply medical curiosity. But if it's the latter—let us pray it is not—then we could be facing what might turn out to be—I don't want to overstate it—a horrifying epidemic."

The phone quivered in Norten's hand as he stared

wide-eyed at the wall. "We must keep this under our hats, professor."

"You think so? I was about to suggest that we send out an urgent alert to obstetricians and others involved with—"

"No, absolutely not. Not until we're sure. We would risk a panic."

"But what if—"

"Continue your excellent work, professor. Don't breathe a word to anyone except me. As the one in charge of the medical aspects of this case, I must assume total responsibility. Mrs. Davis must be approached cautiously, for she is highly suspicious of tests or treatment just now. First, we must have the infant. Then, at the proper time, I will undertake the research into the bodily functions of Mrs. Davis."

"I hope you're right."

"I believe in proceeding with care and caution."

"So many people already dead . . ."

"What's past is past."

"Or prologue, doctor."

≈

The old woman slogged along the dark sidewalk as if through deep sand, lifting her feet wearily, pushing in front of her a twisted, rusting shopping cart loaded with rags. It was for this she was known around town as "the rag lady."

She wore a long, tattered coat, ripped army boots, and a faded kerchief on her head. She muttered to herself as she moved painfully along.

She slept in stairwells or wherever anyone would let her in to curl up behind a door. Though not an esthetic treat, she harmed no one.

Whenever anyone would listen, the rag lady told tales. Stories of things she knew, things she saw: sagas of adventure, visitations of spirits and Martians, insights into the cosmos as well as the immediate neighborhood. Children loved her fables, and would often bring her bits of discarded clothing, which she added to her cart; parents begged them to stay away from her.

All day and into each night, she walked alone, mumbling her own stories over and over again to herself.

She plodded past the playground, where so often she could find an audience. But now she didn't bother looking for anyone, because it was night and the playground was naturally deserted. She trudged steadily on, her head bobbing in rhythm to the slow dirge of her legs.

Until she heard a swing creak.

She pressed her face up against the chain-link fence and tried to focus her watery eyes on the row of swings in the center of the playground. The swing squeaked again and again in regular tempo. Just as it did during the day, when the schoolchildren were there.

Straining to see a distance beyond her normal view, she blinked several times to clear her old, dim eyes. She could make out the swing now, arcing steadily back and forth. And someone in it.

"Halloo," she called weakly.

The swing stopped. The child got off. It came toward her. Not walking, rather half crawling and half hopping. It began to cry.

It neared the fence and stopped, its crying increasing in pitch and intensity. It wailed now, screamed. It sprang onto the fence.

The rag lady's eyes widened slowly in terror. Blood drained from her face. She stumbled backward. "Nooo," she whimpered, "nooo . . ." Her eyes rolled back in her head. She fell across the shopping cart, knocking it over and spilling its contents along the sidewalk.

There she lay, face up, amid all her rags, seeing no longer what now reached the top of the fence and dropped down beside her.

〜

They found her early in the morning.

"Look, sarge, it's the rag lady!"

They pulled the police cruiser to the curb and jumped out. The sergeant quickly knelt at her head and put his hands along the sides of her neck, feeling for pulse.

"She's alive, at least. Call for an ambulance."

The patrolman trotted back to the cruiser to send the call while the sergeant cradled the rag lady's head in his arm.

She stirred and opened her foggy eyes. She threw her hand up as if to ward off a blow, then slowly lowered it as she peered at the sergeant.

"It's okay now, lady, just take it easy. We got an ambulance on its way. Don't try and move."

She moaned and rolled her eyes. "Oooh, ooww . . ."

"On its way, sergeant." The patrolman knelt beside them as they heard the siren in the distance. "What's with her, anyway?"

"Probably hasn't eaten in a week. Take it easy now, lady."

She rocked in his arms and moaned. "I seen it, oooh, I seen it—"

"Yeah, yeah, take it easy, we'll get you into a nice, warm bed."

"Seen what, sergeant? What'd she see?"

"Martian, dinosaur, pot of gold, maybe John Wayne. Who the hell knows? What'd you see, lady?"

She rolled her eyes. "Oooh . . . baby, I seen the baby . . . ooww . . ."

"What baby?"

The ambulance whined around the corner and lurched to a stop. Two white-clad attendants pulled a stretcher out of the back and ran over to where the rag lady lay moaning. Quickly they arranged a pillow and blankets. "Where's she hurt, sergeant?" one of them asked, dropping to his knees beside him.

"Nowhere I can find. I think she just collapsed."

"Okay, ma'am," the attendant said, slipping his arms under her, "nice and easy now, we'll just move you onto the stretcher."

". . . I seen it . . . aaah . . ."

"There, there."

They put her gently on the ambulance bed. One attendant stayed with her, the other closed the doors, and went around to take the driver's seat.

The sergeant waved goodbye and turned toward the cruiser. "Guess we better take her goddam cart," he said to the patrolman. "Stick it in our trunk."

The patrolman picked up the cart. "Sergeant, where's her rags?"

"How the hell should I know? Maybe she sold 'em." He picked up the telephone receiver on the radio. "Dispatcher, this is Car 31, Car 31. Over."

"But who would want to buy—"

"Car 31 . . . Yeah, we got a ten-fifty-four here outside the Darwin School playground, turned out to be the old rag lady . . . Yeah, ambulance just left . . . No visible injuries, like maybe she just passed out . . . Only communication was she kept ranting about seeing something or other . . . Yeah, a baby. Right . . . I don't know, just a baby. Maybe it was Jesus . . . You knew her . . . Yeah. So we'll get back on our ten-ninety-eight . . . What? Resume our patrol, for chrissake. Ain't you got no code chart down there? . . . Right. Ten-four."

≈≈≈

"It was just the old rag lady, lieutenant."

"Yeah, I know," Detective Perkins said, wetting down a fresh cigar, "but what's this about seeing a baby?"

"I don't know. That's all the sergeant said when he radioed in. This is verbatim."

"I don't doubt it," Perkins said, scanning the transcript. "Listen, get him back on the radio, make him repeat exactly what he heard, tell him I said so. I'm going over to the hospital."

"But lieutenant, she wasn't even injured—"

"Just do as I say. You get any more details, call me there."

≈≈≈

Detective Lieutenant Perkins, accompanied by Dr. Norten in his green surgical gear, and Professor Eckstein, hurried along the corridor toward the bed of the rag lady.

"Why the unusual interest, lieutenant?" asked Dr. Norten. "You think she really saw something?"

"You never know."

They entered the room and went quickly to the bedside.

The rag lady was propped up on pillows, clean and pale, her jaw set in sassy disdain for her visitors.

"Now then, missus, I'm Detective Perkins, and you know the doctor here. I understand you saw something last night. Would you tell me about it?"

"Hmmph. I seen it, that's all."

"What?"

"The baby. That monster whippersnapper you been lookin' for."

"Now, dear lady," Dr. Norten cooed, "we all know how you—"

"Tell me what you saw, missus."

She snorted. "Well, if I'm talkin' to a real detective! Lot of folks pretend to be the law. I see lots of things, you know, on my rounds. Nobody believes me nohow."

He flipped open his wallet to reveal his gold shield.

"All right, then. I seen that thing, close up, on the fence. It come right over to me."

"Describe it."

"Well, it didn't look much like nothin' I ever seen before. It had great big eyes, and claws."

"Mmm-hmm. What else? Did it have hair?"

"No hair. Bald as a bowling ball. Funny, round body too, you know? Claws on the legs. I know, 'cause it was grippin' real good on to the fence."

"Mmm-hmm. Did you just find it there, hanging on to the fence?"

"Oh no. It was over there on the swing, swinging up and down. I thought it was maybe one of my friends, one of my many *close* friends. So I called to it. And it come hoppin' right over to the fence."

"Hopping?"

"That's what I said. Like a goshdarn kangaroo. Except farther. It hopped farther, higher."

"Hmm. Did you have any conversation with it?"

"Conversation?"

"Yeah, did it talk to you?"

"Now looka here, you may be a detective, but that don't cut no ice with me if you're gonna wisecrack. How could I talk with a thing like that? I don't even speak French good no more. It just hung there and cried, just like a baby."

"I see."

Dr. Norten took Perkins by the elbow and turned him around and whispered to him, "Detective, I'm afraid you're wasting your time. She could have read all this."

"Mmm. So it just hung there and cried?" Perkins pulled away.

"Cried louder and louder. And then it started up the fence."

"And?"

"Next thing I seen was them policemen and the ambulance fellers."

"What happened to your, unh, belongings?"

"My cart! Where's my cart?" She sat up straight.

"We have your cart, missus, but there was nothing in it."

She shook her head and pursed her lips. "Now that just goes to show ya, can't leave nothing lying around for one minute, somebody up and steals it."

"You think somebody would steal your possessions?"

"Hmmph, these days? You kiddin' me? Why, just the other day I was carrying a shopping bag full of T-bone steaks, with my purse lyin' on top of it, with five hundred dollars in it, and six Mexicans came sidling up to me and started sweet-talkin', and next thing I knew, they run off with my meat and my money."

"See, lieutenant," Dr. North said, smiling sadly, "what we're dealing with here?"

Perkins bowed. "Thank you, missus. Get a good rest now."

"I hope my credit's good. My medical insurance just run out."

≈≈≈

Detective Perkins stood in the hospital corridor and rubbed his chin pensively.

The doctor and the professor stared at their shoes.

"I wonder," Perkins mused, "what happened to her rags."

Professor Eckstein fidgeted with his tie. "Maybe the thing took them."

"Now, professor," Norten said, "I can't believe that *you* take the rag lady seriously. After all, she apparently wasn't even attacked, or hurt in any way."

"Well, perhaps she wasn't a threat to it, once she passed out. And if the thing *was* there, perhaps it took the rags. Perhaps it wanted to build a nest."

"A nest?" Perkins narrowed his eyes.

"Maybe it's getting cold."

"Surely, professor," Dr. Norten said, "if it's gone this long . . . "

Professor Eckstein studied the ceiling. "It could be starting to get cold—if it's running out of adrenaline . . ."

Dr. Norten stepped firmly on the professor's foot.

"What's this about adrenaline?" Detective Perkins asked.

The professor looked back and forth between Perkins and Norten. "Um, well, unh, just that, um, any warm-blooded animal can, ah, run out of energy, and get cold."

"I see." Perkins peered at him and chewed his cigar. "Well, maybe the rag lady didn't see anything at all. Maybe she just left her rags someplace. I've got to get back to the station house. Thank you, gentlemen, for your time."

They watched him walk away toward the front entrance.

"Well, professor," Dr. Norten hissed, "you almost blew it."

"Sorry. Although he's the police, after all, and I thought he should know everything that would help them catch—"

"Not *now,* professor, don't you see? The matter of hormonal balance means nothing to him. That's a matter best left to the medical profession. It has nothing to do with their search for this mutant."

"But I was thinking, doctor, that if this thing thrives according to our thesis, then quite naturally its supply of hormones would tend to be used up when it's on its own. There's only one place it could go to get the vast amounts needed to restore its strength."

"No need to belabor what we already know, professor." The doctor bade him goodbye, then ran into his office to scribble down some hasty notes with a trembling hand.

≋

The United Parcel delivery man handed Frank the large box and he lugged it into the house and put it on the living-room floor.

"My, what's that, darling?" Lenore came into the room wiping her hands with a dish towel.

"From the office. Must be a present of some kind. Heavy."

"Well, go on, open it! I'm excited."

He slit the tape with a letter opener and folded back the flaps. He sat staring at it. "It's my stuff. My office stuff."

"Why would anybody—"

"Pen set, ashtrays, your picture, books—all my stuff."

"Frank . . ."

"I've been kicked out of my office." He shook his head. "I can't believe it."

She knelt beside him on the floor. "Look, there's a note stuck in there."

He opened the envelope and read aloud:

Dear Frank,
Thought it was best for everybody, to close things out this way, without going through all the goodbyes and crap up here that might embarrass you. Everybody here thinks you're terrif, as you know. You're a hell of a PR man, one of the best anywhere, but it just wasn't going to work out any longer staying with our firm, under the circumstances.

I know you'll understand how difficult this decision has been for me. I really can't afford to lose you, but that's the way it goes.

A check for a month's pay will be in the mail to you. You know I'll give you absolutely the highest recommendation whenever you need it. My loss will be somebody else's gain.

My best to Lenore. And please keep in touch, by phone.

Your friend,
Buck Clayton

P.S. I know you must be going through one hell of a trying time right now. Guess it's rough being a parent, although I've never been one—that I know of, ha-ha.

The note slipped from Frank's fingers and fell to the floor. Lenore picked it up and looked at it.

"I don't understand, Frank, I don't understand at all."

He shook his head.

"But he must have said something. You talked to him. You told him you were going to take your vacation. You said everything was all right." Tears were in her eyes.

"I wasn't being quite honest with you, Lenore. It was Buck who insisted I get away for a while. *I* didn't want to go. I wanted to keep working, keep my mind occupied. He made me go. But he never said anything about this."

"But why? Why would he fire you? You had his top accounts."

Frank went to the bar and poured himself some Chivas. He drank it straight and poured some more. "He fired me, Lenore, for public-relations reasons. I should have expected it."

"But you were the best PR man he had—he says it himself."

"He didn't fire me for public-relations *work,* just public-relations *reasons.* With all that has happened, I guess I became a millstone for the company. I would make clients uncomfortable, nervous. And in this business, that's the worst thing you can do, no matter how good your work is. So, along with everything else, our family now has," he drained his drink, "no breadwinner."

"Couldn't you talk to him, Frank, reason with him? Maybe *I* should talk to him. I could explain—"

"No, no, no. I understand it completely. Buck did the right thing, business-wise. I just happen to be the unlucky one lately, falling into one trap after another."

"What do you mean by that?"

"Maybe the hospital PR job's still open. Be a natural for me, even at half the salary I've been making. I'd be a real insider."

"What do you mean by falling into traps?"

He slammed his glass on the bar. "You know goddam good and well what I mean, Lenore! I've worked hard all these years to be good at what I do for a living, and to be a good husband and father. What did I ever do to deserve getting kicked in the belly like this?"

"But, Frank, what did *I* ever do?"

"I don't *know* what you did. Pills, garbage, God-knows-what . . . But whatever you did got you that damn mutated animal that's running around out there killing people! It's already cost me my job, and who knows what else it'll cost me before it's through!"

"But, Frank, you're the *father!*"

"I'm *not* the father! There *is* no father! That thing isn't human! It isn't mine! It's *yours,* Lenore, and it's tearing my life apart!"

"Mine?" She sat staring at him, dumbfounded. Her eyes were dry. She blinked hard a few times, then smiled. "I've got to finish up in the kitchen." She got up and smoothed her hair. "Don't go upstairs just yet, I've got a little more straightening up to do—our bed's still a mess. And then, you know what? I'll make us a nice dinner. How about a roast? Yes." She headed for the kitchen with a bouncy step. "Roast and baked potatoes and lima beans. And maybe I'll whip up a fresh cabbage slaw. We haven't had that in a long time."

"Lenore."

"And before that, just to keep you from starving, I'll mix up an onion dip with celery sticks."

"Lenore!" His eyes were wet.

"Yes, sweetie?"

"I didn't mean what I said."

"What was that, dear?"

In the kitchen, she began pulling out pots and utensils and clanking them onto the stove. "You mean about no breadwinner? Oh, I'm not worried. I have so much confidence in you. With a month to play with, you'll come up with something super—better than what you had." She trotted and twirled in the kitchen, her face flushed, reaching out this way and that to accumulate meat, potatoes, vegetables, and pile them on the counter. "I never thought that Buck Clayton had a big enough operation for you, anyway—no room to grow. He's a lecher, Buck is. Did you know that?" She began chopping up cabbage, her hand a mechanical blur. "He even said something to me once, about getting me alone, showing me a real good time. I'm glad you're out of that place."

Frank came up behind her and closed her in his arms. "Please, Lenore, listen to me, slow down . . ." Her entire body was tense with kinetic energy. "I didn't mean that, about being trapped. I love you so."

She spun from his grasp, then leaned over and gave him a peck on the cheek. "And I love you. Later I'll show you. Right now just let me put this dinner together, okay? Dip'll be ready in a minute. Have you talked to Chris today?"

"He's up at the lake with Charley, you know that. Won't be back until tomorrow."

"Good. Just us. Like honeymooners. You're in my way, lover. Wait in the den, okay? I'll bring the dip to you."

She stood smiling up at him. Then the smile faded, her knees buckled, she tottered backward, and slumped down into a chair. She tilted slowly over, until her head was resting on the table. She shivered.

"What's wrong?" He knelt beside her and put his hand on her head. "Lenore, what is it?"

Her eyes were half closed. "I'm just so tired, Frank, and cold."

He hugged her. "But all of a sudden like that?"

"I'm sorry. I've been so up and down lately. My head is spinning. I'm not dizzy, exactly. Confused. Sometimes I feel like I'm floating outside myself, like my body's not my own."

"You've exhausted yourself. And I haven't helped at all. Come on, let me get you into bed. I'm so sorry for the things I said, for thinking only of myself, for being such a weakling. I'll carry you up."

"No, I'm okay. I'll go up myself. This usually passes in a few minutes."

He took her arm and helped her up the stairs and tucked her into bed. He kissed her on the forehead and went back down to sit in the den. He poured a drink and sprawled out in the soft chair and fell asleep.

Sometime later in the night the phone rang. Frank answered it groggily.

"Mr. Davis? This is Lieutenant Perkins. Sorry to be bothering you so late, but it's important. Could you meet me right away over at the Darwin School? There's something here I'd like you to see, and ask you about. Just tell my men at the front door you're here to see me."

≋

It stemmed, in a way, from one of those minor school-board matters. Having to cut back on their budget, they had sliced out funds for the night watchman, letting the old man go, after all those years, with a Good Citizen plaque and a small pension. But then, after a series of incidents of petty vandalism, they had installed in the lower windows—at slightly higher cost than to retain the watchman—a silent alarm system hooked up directly to police headquarters.

And so, when entry was made tonight through one of the first-floor windows, the police had been instantly alerted, and cars arrived on the scene within minutes.

Before the cars arrived, one of the many foot patrolmen assigned to each block of Westwood and vicinity during the several days' search for the monster-baby responded to a message on his walkie-talkie and ran around the corner to the dark, square, two-story brick school. Following instructions, he didn't go in, but scouted the windows from the outside. He quickly found one open and heard noises inside: the tinkling of a music box, the rattling of blocks, the rolling of plastic wheels across the floor.

Eight cars quickly converged on the scene, their sirens silent. Three were locals, and five State Troopers.

Most of the men fanned out to encircle the building. Detective Perkins took a small unit to the front door, followed closely by Captain Sanford and a handful of Troopers.

"Step aside, lieutenant," the captain said, "my men'll blow that door right off its hinges."

"No need." Perkins nodded to one of his men, who stooped at the door with a tiny tool, quickly slipped the lock, and shoved the door open.

"Okay," Perkins said quietly, "stay together until I tell you to split up. Keep your mouths shut and easy on your trigger fingers."

They entered the building, the local policemen holdin their revolvers at their shoulders pointed up, the Troopers cradling their shotguns. They spread out along the main hallway.

"Where the hell's the lights?" came a whisper. "Wall switches don't work."

"Must be turned off by some master switch, automatically timed. Use your flashlights."

Beams from a dozen flashlights sprayed around the

yellow walls, into open classrooms; heavy breathing from a dozen men filled the hall.

"Brunt. Where's Patrolman Brunt?"

"Right here, lieutenant," he whispered back.

"What room was it where you heard the noise?"

"I think it must be right down here, third door on the right."

The door was closed. Detective Perkins slowly turned the knob and eased it open. Lights played around the room, covering every corner. Nothing moved.

Perkins and three of his men edged inside. Toys were strewn all over the room. A hand-painted poster that said, "Darwin Kindergarten," with flowers and a sun on it, lay on the floor. Perkins stumbled over a tiny merry-go-round that responded with a few dying notes of its song.

"That's it, lieutenant, that's what I heard."

With his foot, Perkins sent a fire engine rolling across the wooden floor.

"That too."

Again with his foot, he pushed over a pile of blocks.

"Yeah, that's it. Somebody was in here, all right."

"Or thing."

"Yeah."

"Not here now."

"If it was," came the hoarse growl of Captain Sanford, "we'd have it plastered all over the wall before it could say A-B-C."

"You stayed right outside the window, Brunt?" Perkins asked.

"Yes sir, just like you said, all the time until the men had the building surrounded."

"So maybe it's still in here."

"I sure hope so," muttered Sanford.

"You got all your men together, captain?"

"Sent 'em on ahead, spread 'em to reconnoiter the ground floor."

"I thought I said to—"

"Every one of my men is like a guerrilla fighter, lieutenant, handle himself in any situation."

Detective Perkins gritted his teeth. "Okay, let's seal off this room. We'll take the rooms one by one, check 'em, seal 'em off."

"Lieutenant, look at this!"

Perkins aimed his light. The patrolman was on one knee beside the poster. Next to him several small bottles of paints were tipped over. And from these blobs of paint, which the patrolman now pointed at, were several tracks of drying color, tracks resembling the spoor of a very large bird.

"It musta walked in this stuff, lieutenant! It left a trail!"

Several flashlight beams converged on the tracks and moved slowly along them, toward the men themselves. The tracks—mixtures of faint blue, gold, and red—passed directly under them. The men stepped aside, their lights tracing the tracks out the door and down the hallway.

The men stood where they were, allowing their flashlight beams to move farther and farther along the hallway away from them, toward the broad stairway at the end.

"Any of your men upstairs, captain?"

Sanford flashed his light around behind him, at the men herded together. "Nope. All here again, as ordered."

"Except Darcey, captain," came a voice from the rear. "Trooper Darcey maybe went up."

Perkins snapped his head around to the captain. "Jesus!"

"He'll be all right. Top man. Anything's up there, he'll get it."

The two leaders moved slowly down the hallway, the others bunched up behind them, all tilting their lights to see the poster paint, bird-like tracks reaching out ahead of them, but growing fainter, on the floor.

They reached the foot of the stairs and stopped to shine their lights up. The tracks had disappeared; the paint was gone. Halfway up was a landing, and the stairs doubled back over their heads.

"Darcey?" Perkins called softly. "Trooper Darcey?"

"If he's on the job, lieutenant, stalking something up there, he won't answer."

"Maybe he didn't go up there, captain," somebody said. "Maybe he went outside. He said he needed to take a leak."

Detective Perkins started upward, the others pressed behind him. They reached the landing and stopped. Perkins held up his hand. There wasn't a sound. They then made the turn and went up the last section of stairs to the top. The men gathered and all shined their lights down the long hall.

Nothing.

Captain Sanford leaned back into the group. "Couple you Troopers go on back down. Go outside, see if Darcey's out there. Ask our men out there if they saw anybody go out."

"Yes sir."

Two Troopers trotted down the stairs.

"Okay. Room by room," Perkins commanded. "Captain, take your Troopers down the left side. We'll take the right."

The captain nodded and motioned his men forward to the first room on the left.

Detective Perkins panned his light down the hall, then flashed in at the first room on the right. The door was open. All the classroom doors were open. He started toward the first room. He stopped and flashed his light down the hall again.

Except one room. Fourth down on the right. The door was closed.

Perkins held up his hand, then just one finger, and slowly brought it down to point at that closed door. His men fell in beside him, walking softly, heel-and-toe.

Perkins spread his arms and stopped them. "Everybody got their safeties off?" he whispered.

He heard one click, and scowled.

He began moving forward again.

From outside came a hoarse, whispered call, "Troopers!" followed by the thudding steps of running boots, then more whispers.

"What the hell they doing out there?" Perkins murmured.

They listened.

"He's asking them if they seen Darcey, lieutenant."

Perkins snatched a cigar from his jacket pocket and stuck it in his mouth.

They were at the closed door. Perkins put his hand on the knob, then took his hand off and stepped back. He slowly brought his right foot up to the level of his belly, then smashed it against the door, breaking the latch and slamming the door open against the wall, the crash echoing through the school.

Lights shined straight ahead.

"Window's open."

He edged in along the shattered door, running his light quickly around the room. Then down, under the window, on the floor.

No more caution. His men burst into the room and dropped to the side of the uniformed body whose fresh blood was spilling from the gouge in his throat and oozing along the baseboard.

"He ain't ours, lieutenant," one of Perkins's men called out.

Captain Sanford and his men poured into the room and dashed to the fallen figure. "No, he ain't yours. Ours. Darcey."

Perkins lunged for the window and leaned out. Drainpipe just to his left, half pulled away from the brick. Tracks on it, sliding, red. Not paint, blood. He looked down at the ground. "Where the hell's the Troopers was supposed to be on this side of the building?" he roared.

They came running over the grass from the front. "We're here, sir, just checking on one of our men."

Sanford leaned out the window beside Perkins. "So it went out the window and down the pipe."

"Yeah."

"And my men weren't covering the ground."

"Nope."

"I'll have to take responsibility for that."

"Don't tell *me* about it, captain, goddam it! Tell your men about their buddy!"

State and local policemen stood staring down where the beams of their flashlights covered the body of their slaughtered comrade.

"Okay," Detective Perkins chomped down hard on his cigar, "somebody find me a phone. I can't wait no longer. I gotta get Davis up here and ask him some things."

≈≈≈

Frank arrived at the school to see flashlight beams waving around the playground and in nearby lawns and shrubbery. He went to the front door, where he was confronted by two policemen standing with legs apart and nightsticks in front of them.

"I'm Frank Davis, here to see Detective Perkins. What's going on out there?"

"Afraid you'll have to ask Lieutenant Perkins about that, sir. We aren't allowed to answer any questions."

"I passed an ambulance on the way here. Anything to do with this?"

"I'll show you to Lieutenant Perkins, sir, he's right inside."

Perkins was seated at the principal's desk, surrounded by several aides manning communications equipment. Captain Sanford slumped on a chair in the corner.

Perkins nodded to Frank and motioned to a chair.

"What's going on around here, lieutenant? What was that ambulance doing?"

"I'm afraid the school had a visitor, Mr. Davis. I'm afraid it was your kid."

Frank squirmed. "I wish you wouldn't refer to it that way."

"I know you don't like it, Mr. Davis, but it's time we all faced up to a few things. I didn't call you over here because you were just an interested bystander, you know."

"I know. You got it, then? It was in the ambulance?"

"No. We ain't got it. Close, but no cigar." Which reminded him to take out a fresh one and jam it between his teeth. "It was a cop in the ambulance. Trooper. One of Captain Sanford's men there."

"I'm sorry, captain. Was he hurt bad?"

Captain Sanford turned his face to the wall.

"Dead like the others," Perkins said. "Throat carved out. Killed him upstairs, slid down a drainpipe, and got away across the grounds somewhere."

Frank stared at him, stunned. "So it's still out there."

"Tell me about it, Davis. Look, I haven't brought you into this much before now, because I didn't want to upset you any more than you are, and also because frankly I didn't think you could help us that much. Maybe you can't. But I want to go over a few things with you, just between us."

"Okay. Could you make it quick, lieutenant? I left my wife at home alone, you know."

"I know. We're keeping an eye on the place."

"I hope your men aren't stomping around outside. It'll scare her to death. And you better not have sent them inside either, because we don't want anybody—"

"I know all that. They're keeping an eye on it, that's all. She won't even know they're there. Let's take a little walk, you and me."

They left the office and walked down the hall. Detective Perkins nodded at his man stationed outside the kindergarten room, and he and Frank went inside and closed the door behind them.

Lights were now on in the school. Perkins just stood and let Frank's eyes wander over the room.

"Well, what about it, lieutenant? What am I supposed to see?"

"This the room where your wife taught?"

"Yeah. Not full-time. Substitute. But when she was at the school, this is where she worked."

"How often?"

"Maybe once a week, or less. Until the regular teacher got sick. She's been here quite a bit lately. She changed it a lot, improved it, She cared a lot about——"

"How changed it?"

"Well, the toys, for example. She's responsible for most of the stuff you see here. They used to have a lot of junk for the kids to play with: old metal toys, broken stuff, dirty things that had been here for years. There never seemed to be enough money for modern toys, good ones. But, see, I have this account in my public-relations business——or had the account. It was a toy company. And we were able to have the school get a whole bunch of new toys at discount. It's just like what we have at home. My boy's eleven now, but he used to play with stuff just like this. In fact, seeing all these things is like walking into his old room at home."

"Yeah?"

"Yeah. Something wrong with that?"

"Nope. But this is the room that thing came to. This is where my man first heard it. Like it was playing with this stuff." Detective Perkins knelt and shoved some of the blocks and trucks around. He picked up the merry-go-round and wound it up. He held it while it played its song.

"My son's got the same one."

"Yeah? Interesting."

"Well, if it's anything like a real human kid, it probably likes to play with toys."

"Yeah. When's the last time you or any member of your family was in this room?"

"Well, Chris goes to school here, but I doubt that he'd come into this room. Let's see. My wife was pregnant, as you know, but they waived the rules to let her keep coming in, since the regular teacher was sick. She worked pretty much right up until recently. I don't know the last day."

"Okay."

"Look, if you're telling me she had something to do with—"

"When I want to tell you something, I'll tell you, Mr. Davis. I'm just asking, at this point in time. Just asking. Don't read too much into it. Let's go upstairs."

Men were posted outside every room. Frank and Detective Perkins went into the room where the body of the Trooper had been found.

"He was right over there, under that window, Mr. Davis." Bloodstains were still evident. "The window was open. Come over here." They leaned out the window together. "See this drainpipe? Now, you and I couldn't reach it from here. But see the blood on it? That's the way the kid got down. Then it musta just took off."

"After you were already here?"

"Right."

"But why didn't you have men outside—"

"We can't be everywhere. It got by us. We don't know exactly how." A score of men were scouring the yards and driveways in the neighborhood. "It's probably not in the immediate area any longer. We found a little blood on the grass right down there."

"Why don't you use dogs?"

"Tried dogs. They get confused. They just want to follow the scent of the blood, and that down there ain't the blood of the thing we're after. If it had a lot of blood on it, they *could* track it that way. But it just had a little on its feet, and it disappeared after it hit the ground. Either that thing don't have no scent of its own, or it's not a scent the dogs go for. And we haven't got anything from the thing to wave in front of their noses."

He pulled back in from the window and leaned against the wall, chewing on his cigar. "So now, all of this give you any ideas?"

"Me? How? Am I supposed to have it figured out somehow?"

"Nope. Just wondering what you thought."

"What I *thought!* Jesus! I think you better catch it, that's all."

"It ain't leaving town, apparently."

"No."

"And it seems to me it's getting kind of bold."

"How? Because it came into the school?"

"That, and what maybe happened the night before. You know the rag lady?"

"Everybody does."

"Well, she says she saw the thing the night before, swinging in the playground."

"You believe her?"

"I don't know."

"Did it attack her?"

"Nope."

"Well, why not?"

"Mr. Davis, I don't know why it does attack, or why it doesn't."

"But the rag lady dreams up all kinds of—"

"Look, if you suddenly came in here today from New York City, and I told you this whole story of what's been going on around here, you'd figure I was dreaming. This whole goddam mess is like somebody's science-fiction dream. So I'm very careful about what I laugh off."

"I understand."

"So I ain't saying she saw it, I ain't saying she didn't. But one night she says she saw it in the playground, the next night it's in the school, right next door. I'd say that's getting bold."

"I . . . see."

"Somebody at the hospital yesterday said something about it might be getting cold."

"Why?"

"It mighta took the rag lady's rags. They were gone. Maybe to build a nest, a guy said, something about adrenaline, needing adrenaline."

"Then do they know something about its physical makeup?"

"I don't know. How's your wife lately?"

"Tired, naturally. Upset. Depressed."

"Cold?"

"Hey, come on, lieutenant! What're you trying to say? When people get over-tired they almost always feel cold. You trying to make some kind of ghost story out of this? Some kind of supernatural nonsense?"

"Nope. Some kind of natural nonsense. I wish it *was* a ghost story. I ain't a doctor, but it seems to me that the thing must have something from both of you in it, something of your makeup, your genes, your blood, your brains—something."

"Now, dammit! I don't have to listen to that! Everybody's trying to make us into monsters. This isn't a damn human kid!"

"It ain't a raisin either, Mr. Davis. It ain't a dream and it ain't a Martian."

"But that's just the kind of talk that gets spread around, starts rumors that we're weirdos, cost me my job—"

"You lost your job over this?"

Frank stared out the window, his eyes heavy with fatigue. "Yeah. You can't be in public relations with this kind of cloud hanging over your head."

"Sorry to hear that. But it's for just that reason that *I* haven't spread this kind of talk."

"You haven't?"

"Nope. Not to anybody. Like I said, this is just between you and me."

"But I don't understand. I thought you said you were talking to people at the hospital about—"

"Listening, Mr. Davis, just listening. My job ain't to tell stories, or to gossip. But my job *is* to listen, to everything and everybody. I been a cop for twenty years. I solve my cases. I don't blabber about it. If I have suspicions, I tell them only to those of my men who need to know. I keep things to myself until I'm sure. Right now my job is to catch whatever kind of thing we're after. I ain't sure what it is, where it is, or what it's gonna do next. I ain't sure about anything. That's why I'm still listening to everything. You've been helpful."

"How?"

"I ain't sure."

≈

The ambulance was an old model, kept along with the newer ones because its unusually high undercarriage allowed it to pass over old rutted roads or up into canyon gullies where the more recent, low-slung models would get hung up. It was used on the school call, to transport the dead Trooper to the morgue, because the other ambulances were out on two traffic accidents and a heart attack.

Since it often picked up a hunk of brush or a branch on its chassis during one of its out-back calls, the driver did not think it unusual and did not pay much attention to the fact that, when he parked it in the garage at the hospital, something seemed to be hanging underneath, its shadow protruding slightly at the rear. He would slide under the ambulance tomorrow and pull off the branch or whatever.

He stepped outside and started to pull down the sliding door of the garage when he heard something clump to the floor inside. There was a crash of glass.

He flung the door back up, just as a pale form hurtled through the side window of the garage. "AAAYYAA!" he screamed as he backed away.

Several people ran out of the hospital. "Through the window!" he gasped, pointing. "It went through the window!"

They ran to the window and looked out. Lawn and hedges and street. Nothing else to be seen. They shook their heads.

"How'd you break the window, McGurk?" asked one of the doctors.

"I didn't break it! The thing! That thing jumped through there!"

"Where's your bottle, McGurk? Finish it already?"

"Oh, darn it, I ain't drunk!"

The doctor leaned close to him and sniffed. "You don't smell too bad. You on vodka now?"

"That thing went through the window."

"Sure. Why don't you just stay out here? Maybe it'll come back."

"Hey, I don't get paid for ambulance driving, you know. I'm telling the cops about this."

"Go ahead. Use the pay phone."

※

Detective Lieutenant Perkins got on his knees and stuck his head under the rear bumper of the ambulance. He reached in and felt, then brought out his hand and sniffed it. He got up and looked at the jagged edges of the garage window. Then he walked outside, followed by McGurk. He knelt and studied the shards of glass on the hospital lawn. He picked one piece up and sniffed it.

"Lemme see your hands, McGurk."

McGurk held out his hands, and Perkins took the fingers and looked at them, tracing the lines like a palm reader. "Hmm. Clean."

"Of course they're clean. So what?"

"There's grease on some of these glass fragments, McGurk, that's all. What'd you say the thing looked like?"

"Little—a lot smaller than you or me. Just jumped straight through there."

"What would you say it looked like?"

"I didn't. And I won't. I'm not letting you laugh at me."

Detective Perkins leaned slowly toward him until his face was an inch away. "Look close, McGurk. Am I laughing?"

"No sir." McGurk leaned backward.

"Am I smiling?"

"No sir."

Perkins grabbed his shoulders, squeezing them hard. " 'No sir' is right, McGurk, I ain't laughing. I ain't even smiling. I'm frowning, McGurk. That means I'm *serious*, McGurk!"

McGurk choked. "It looked kind of like a *baby*, officer. But bigger, and with a big head, I think."

Perkins flung him aside and stomped off to the cruiser. He settled in beside his driver, scowling, his teeth grating around his cigar.

"Well, what do you think, lieutenant?"

"Aaargh!"

The driver gulped. "Sorry."

"I'll ask your dumb questions for you. Why would the thing come back to the hospital?"

"Well, yes."

"How the hell would I know, you bushy-tailed rookie? Maybe it thought it was coming home!"

≫≫≫

Frank, in his robe, shuffled out to the kitchen. "Morning."

"Hi, darling." Lenore, dressed in slacks, her milk-filled breasts arching under her sweater, hugged him. "You should have waked me up when you came in last night."

"You knew I was out?"

"I heard you come in. Out for a walk, I assumed, right?"

"I didn't want to disturb you, you needed the sleep, so I just curled up on the couch."

She measured some coffee grounds and dumped them into the top of the electric percolator. "You don't look like you slept a wink. Maybe some of those pills the doctor prescribed for me . . ."

"I'm fine." He rubbed his chin, his hand rasping over the stubble. "Guess I should shave."

"Not for my sake." She broke some eggs into the skillet. "Oh look, double yolk. That means good luck."

"Yeah. I'll go get dressed."

"You don't have to, you know, you could just take it easy for today."

"No, I know. But I might as well."

"Before you go, would you mind bringing in the milk?"

"Okay." He walked to the front door and gathered up the six bottles, making two trips. "We got a new milkman?"

"I don't know. Why?"

"I thought I left a note yesterday, just two bottles, since Chris isn't here. Maybe I didn't."

"It'll keep. Chris'll be home tomorrow maybe, or the day after."

"Maybe." He opened the refrigerator door. It was well-stocked. He moved some things to make room for the milk, and put the bottles in. He couldn't fit the bread in after the milk. The freezer was full too, but he jammed some of the frozen meat back to the rear and stuffed in the bread. "We could feed an army."

"Makes such a difference when we don't have regular meals, when Chris is away. Would you like a rib roast tonight, or chateaubriand?"

He slammed the doors to the refrigerator and freezer. "I don't care."

"What's the matter? Did I say something wrong?"

"No, no. I really don't care, both sound good. It's just me. I could use some sleep. Maybe you're right. Maybe I could use a sedative, knock me out for a few hours."

"They're upstairs by our bed." She poured two cups of coffee, then came over and put her arms around him. "You've been right too, Frank darling. About how we have to get back to normal, the standard routines that help you get through bleak periods. I'm trying, I really am."

"I know. Maybe you're trying too hard. You don't have to fire around making fancy meals and all that."

"I want to, makes me feel better. I had the chills last night, but today I feel terrific."

"Lenore, when were you at the school last?"

"Couple weeks ago, I guess. The other teacher came back—good thing too. Why?"

"Just wondered."

"If you're worried about the money, we'll be all right. You have your month's salary. And in a couple of days I'll be able to go back, if they need me."

"No, it's nothing. Just small talk."

"I know. Isn't it strange how we miss that, just chatting? So much has gone on, so much serious talk, we haven't had any time to just chat. I think it's time we brought our son home, don't you? I miss him."

"So do I. But not just yet. He's better off where he is." He started out of the kitchen.

"Don't you want your eggs?"

"Not now, thanks. Sorry you wasted them. I'm just dead on my feet." He dragged himself up the stairs.

"Be careful with those pills," she called. "You're not used to them. They're strong."

He went to the bathroom and drew a glass of water. On his way to the bedroom, he stopped at the nursery. Opening the door, he looked in, seeing the cozy crib and the toys neatly placed in the corner of the room. He closed his eyes and pulled the door shut.

He found the pill bottle on the nightstand, read the label, tapped one out on his hand, and swallowed it.

He sipped some water, then tapped out another one and swallowed that. He emptied his glass, pulled off his robe and sank onto the bed. He pulled the covers high up around him, and fell into a deep, dizzy sleep.

Lenore took two eggs from the skillet and put them on her plate, next to two pieces of bacon and two slices of toast. She drained a glass of orange juice and poured another. She sat down, inhaling with pleasure the aroma of her food. As she started to eat, the cat jumped up on the table beside her and sniffed at her plate. Lenore cut off some small pieces and put them on a separate plate and set it on the floor at her feet. The cat began eating voraciously.

"Seems like years, right, Biscuit? So hungry."

She finished her plate, then took it to the stove and reloaded it with Frank's portions, poured some more orange juice, refilled her coffee cup, and sat back down. She chewed the bacon slowly, savoring it.

"I can just feel the energy flowing back into me, Biscuit. Too bad you don't like coffee. It's a marvelous stimulant. I feel like I could move a mountain."

A drop of coffee dribbled onto her chest. She daubed it with a napkin, and stared down at her breasts, so large and ready to feed a baby.

A tear rolled down her cheek. Brushing it away, she stood up, forced a smile, and broke two more eggs into the skillet.

≈≈≈

Frank dreamed savage dreams. He was chasing a tiny crab. Then the crab was chasing him, but now it was huge.

Then he was a doctor, dressed in a surgical gown, ordering nurses around. But every time he spoke sharply, a nurse's throat began to bleed. Not blood, but milk poured down her neck.

Then he was lying on an operating table. They wanted him to give birth. He tried to tell them he wasn't the mother. They said it was a large baby, looking just like him.

Then he was making love to somebody, somebody with his secretary's face. Mary kept saying to him, "Mr. Clayton wants to see you now . . ." But he wasn't making love to her. He was strangling her. Her face became Lenore's. And *she* was strangling *him*.

Then he was in court. They were charging him with not paying a parking ticket. He wasn't allowed to say anything. They sentenced him to three weeks in St. Thomas, and handed him a key.

Then he was sitting on the living-room floor next to a large cardboard box. The box was crying like a baby. He opened it. There was a baby inside. A beautiful tiny baby. He picked it up and hugged it. It became a crab. A huge crab. It chased him around the room, calling to him, "Mr. Clayton wants to see you now . . ."

He woke. He stared at the ceiling. The sheets were wet with his perspiration. Turning his head toward the bedside table, he could barely see it. It was night, the room was dark.

The house was quiet. He blinked. He sat up, rubbing his head. He had a headache. His left leg was asleep and he shook it, feeling the needles of returning blood stab into it.

He felt for his slippers, found them with his toes. They were facing toward his feet. He wiggled them around, finally fitting them on, and rose, felt dizzy, sat back down, got up, stood for a moment, and headed for the bathroom.

He picked up his watch from the dressing table. "Jesus, slept all day."

He doused water on his face, and brushed his teeth. He looked into the mirror. "Shave." He reached into the medicine cabinet and took out the can of foam, shook it, and sprayed out a glob and rubbed it on his face. He peered into the mirror at his eyes, red-rimmed, baggy. "Headache." Opening the bottle of Bufferin, he tossed down two tablets.

He heard a door close downstairs.

He walked out of the bathroom to the head of the stairs. "Lenore?" He cupped his hand around his mouth to call again, and felt the foam. He went back to finish shaving.

Returning to the bedroom, he found his bathrobe. It was under the covers. "Wonder what else I took to bed with me." He sat on the bed for a minute, wishing his head would clear. Then he went downstairs.

≋

The only light was from the small, red-shaded lamp in the den. "Lenore?" He switched on the light in the living room, then the kitchen. "Lenore?" She go out or what?

He checked the back door. The bolt was in place. And the front door. The locks were closed and the safety chain in its slot.

"Come on, Lenore, where are you?"

The guest bathroom, off the den. He went through the living room into the den and saw that the bathroom door was closed. "Lenore? You in there?" He tried it. It wasn't locked. She wasn't in there.

"For chrissake!"

Back in the living room, he flicked on the TV. Cartoons. "Sesame Street" or some goddam thing. He changed channels. News. Lakers lost to the Knicks, 111–103. Clear, sunny, cool tomorrow. Stay tuned for the movie. He switched to the "Tonight Show." Surely they would bust into that if they had a news flash.

Damm it! Doesn't anybody care what the hell is happening around here? What do they do, bury it in the middle of the news, give it thirty seconds and then move on to the damn basketball scores? He hissed through his teeth and plopped down in the chair in front of the TV.

Something touched his shoulder, and he sprang up. "Lenore!"

"You feeling better now?" She smiled calmly.

"You scared the crap outta me!"

"I'm sorry, dear."

"I called you, a hundred times!"

"I didn't hear you. What're you watching?"

"Where've you been? I called you."

"Straightening up. What's the matter, are you cranky because you just woke up?" She smiled and patted his cheek.

"Where? I called you all over. You weren't downstairs."

"Darling, I've been all over the house. You don't realize how much there is to do."

"I mean just now. When I was calling you. Where were you just now?"

She stared at him, stonily. "Chris's room."

"You couldn't hear me in there?"

"Evidently not."

"But *I* heard *you* downstairs, when I was in the bathroom."

She picked up the *TV Guide*. "Mind if I switch? There's a very good movie tonight. Paul Newman."

"Go ahead. I can't look at TV. My eyes hurt. My whole head's coming apart." He winced and rubbed his stomach. "I need something to calm me down."

"Shall I make you a drink?"

"No, no thanks. Excuse me."

She went over to the TV. Frank went into the kitchen.

He opened the refrigerator and reached in automatically, without looking, taking a bottle of milk. He took a glass from the cabinet and sat down at the table. The milk bottle was almost empty. He poured the ounce or two that was left and drank it. Then he got up to get another bottle.

His feet clanked against bottles on the floor by the sink. He stooped to straighten up the ones he had knocked over. Five milk bottles, all empty.

He opened the refrigerator. No more milk.

Not much of anything.

He stood gazing at the half-empty shelves. "Lenore? Has Chris been here today?"

No answer.

He walked into the living room, where Lenore was watching the movie. "Lenore, I said has Chris been here today?"

"No, of course not," she said without turning her head. "Why do you ask?"

"You wouldn't fib to me? I know you wanted him back. But I had a good reason. So now I'm asking—"

"Dear, I haven't been out of the house all day. If he had been here, I would have known it. And certainly I would have told you."

There was an edge to her voice that he didn't like. But then, he had practically accused her of lying. He rubbed his growling belly. "I'm going to get dressed."

He went upstairs to the bedroom and quickly pulled on his shirt and pants and shoes. He guessed he had slept too much. He felt lousy. Nervous. High-strung. Now he wouldn't be able to sleep all night. She had the TV on too loud. She was laughing.

He hated checking up on her. He hated doing anything sneaky. But he wanted to know.

He walked down the hall to Chris's room and turned on the light. A mess. Sports equipment all over the floor. Books down from the shelves.

He needed a drink, after all.

He walked past Lenore in the living room. "I wish someone would respect my feelings around here," he muttered.

She ignored him. She was cackling at some kind of cartoon or puppets, what he had first turned on.

He reached over her to turn the sound down. "Why are you looking at that junk? I thought you were going to watch the movie."

She didn't answer. She simply leaned forward and turned up the volume.

Frank went into the den and poured several ounces of Chivas. He picked up the phone and dialed. "Hello, Charley?"

"Hi. That you, Frank?"

"Yeah. Hey listen, Charley, is Chris okay? You been with him all day?"

"Sure, Frank, he's fine. He's right here in the room watching TV, so I gotta keep my voice down. We had a great time at the lake. What's up? You okay?"

"Yeah, we're okay."

"I had one hell of a time keeping him away from the newscasts and papers and all, today. But he doesn't know anything. His teacher sent over his schoolwork. You've really got a good kid, Frank, you should be grateful."

"I am, Charley, believe me, I am. You've been with him all the time, then?"

"We're like two peas in a pod, Frank. Together every minute."

"He hasn't been back here, to our house? I mean, he couldn't have slipped out and come back here, for a little while?"

"Hey, buddy, you don't doubt me, do you? I know how important this is. I wouldn't let you down—not ever, but especially now. We just got back this morning from the fishing trip. I made him lunch, we played Parcheesi, ordered in a pizza for supper. I sat here with him while he did his homework—until all the newscasts were over. Then I let him watch TV. That's what he's doing now. You want to hear more?"

"Forgive me, Charley. I'm sorry I asked. My nerves lately. You're a very special friend."

"You can relax as far as he's concerned, Frank. He's fine—anxious to come home, of course, but fine. Want to talk to him?"

"No, not just now. I'll see you—"

Charley laid the receiver on the table before he

heard Frank's last words. He called, "Chris, your Dad wants to talk to you."

Chris jumped to the phone. "Dad? Hi, Dad! When can I come home?"

"Chris, you haven't been back here today, have you? You didn't run out on Charley and slip back here today, just for a few minutes?"

"I don't know what you mean, Dad. You told me to stay with Charley. Don't you trust me? Don't we always trust each other?"

"Sure, Chris, I'm sorry. I didn't mean anything. I'm a little tired, that's all."

"Can I talk to Mom?"

"Not just now, son. She's asleep. It'd be better if I didn't wake her."

"Is she okay? Is the baby home from the hospital yet? When do I get to see him? It's a boy, isn't it? . . . Dad? Dad?"

Chris looked at the receiver, which now sent out a dial tone. He handed it to Charley, who put it to his ear for a moment, then hung it up.

Chris looked at the floor. "He didn't even say goodbye."

"That's okay, Chris, it's okay." He put his arm around the boy. "He's just tired. You didn't hear him say goodbye."

"What did I do? Did I say something wrong? Was he angry because I asked if it was a boy?"

"No, no, of course not. That special over on TV? You hungry? Come on, let's go warm up the rest of that pizza."

"No thanks. I think I'll go to bed."

"Good idea, Chris. It's late. Been a long day."

Chris reached the foot of the stairs and turned back. "I'm not mad at you or anything, Charley, I just feel like going to bed."

"I know. Go ahead. I'll be up in a few minutes to tuck you in."

Chris went into the guest bedroom and closed the door. He didn't turn on the light. He crossed to the window and lifted it slowly open. He turned back toward the door and listened. He could hear Charley moving around in the kitchen.

He leaned out the window. In the dark, he could just make out the large tree nearby, and the branch that brushed the house next to the window. He put one leg over the sill and reached for the branch. He got hold of it with both hands and looked down at the shadowy ground below.

Pulling himself inch by inch out of the window, he finally let his feet dangle free. He hung from the branch, which dipped and swayed with his weight. Carefully, hand over hand, he worked his way to the crotch where the branch joined the trunk. He climbed onto the trunk and squatted down, looking back at the window.

Still no light in there; Charley was still downstairs.

He shimmied down the trunk, dropped to the lawn, scrambled to his feet, and took off running through the backyard in the direction of his home.

≈≈≈

Frank stared numbly at his drink on the bar. A line of sweat formed just under his hair along his forehead. He started to take a drink. Ice.

He went to the freezer and pulled it open. He reached in for the ice cubes, felt them under his fingers, then stopped.

The freezer shelves were almost empty. Most of the meat was gone.

He let his hand slide off the ice cubes, stepped back, and let the door wheeze shut by itself. He stared at the closed freezer.

He put his drink down by the sink and hurried out to Lenore. She was laughing quietly, swaying back and forth. On TV now was a commercial for Chevrolet.

"Lenore," he took her shoulders, "Lenore, Lenore, please . . ."

She continued chuckling and swaying back and forth. Frank released her, staring at the back of her head as she swayed.

No, please no.

He glanced around the room, then at the stairs. He went to the stairs and started quickly up, then slowed, taking each step quietly, listening, looking up at the upstairs hallway.

When he reached the last step, he stood silently, holding his breath, staring at the closed door of the nursery.

≈≈≈

"All set?" Charley looked up the stairs. "Ready to be tucked in?" He listened. Probably asleep already. He turned back toward the living room, then hesitated. No, I promised him I would be up.

He went softly up the steps and into the guest bedroom. He tiptoed to the bed and put his hand gently on the covers. Then he put both hands on, finally slapped all around.

"Chris, you in the bathroom?"

He leaned into the hallway. The bathroom door was open. No light on.

"Chris?"

He saw the open window. "Oh no—!" He ran to it and looked out. "No, Chris—"

He flew down the stairs and out to the garage; he yanked on the door of the old station wagon. Stuck as usual. Finally he wrestled it open. He jumped in and ground the starter until it caught at last, rammed the gears into reverse, churned out of the garage, squealed into forward on the street, and roared off toward the Davis house.

≋

Chris felt like an animal, excited, tense, watchful, scared. He crouched under a bush, trying to stem his breathing, his heart pumping wildly. So many policemen around. Why? Were they already looking for him?

He knew the ones on the corner had almost seen him. That was the worst part, the most difficult part, crossing the streets. He had made it three times. Just one more street to go.

A breeze rustled through the bushes and trees. Chris was glad. They wouldn't notice his movements.

They shouldn't be looking for him—it wasn't wrong to be going home. But they might think it was. They wouldn't hurt him, but they would stop him. They would take him back to Charley's. Charley would be sad. He wouldn't understand.

He liked Charley. Very much. He didn't want to hurt him. He would explain it to him later. Or Dad would. Dad would understand, Dad always understood everything. Except now. Now Dad didn't seem to want to talk to him, didn't want to see him, didn't want him to come home. Maybe Mom would. He hoped Mom would be happy to have him home.

Anyway, it wasn't wrong to be going to his own home. He wouldn't be doing it, if it was wrong.

Something *was* wrong, though. Something was so wrong that it forced him to climb out of the window at Charley's and run to his own house. Forced him to. He didn't know what it was. He couldn't figure it out, what made him do this. Just something he felt. Something pulled him. Like love, maybe. He was drawn by how much he loved Mom and Dad, and how much something didn't seem right about them right now, something that scared him. He loved them so much that he started to cry, soundlessly, his tears rolling down his face and his neck, making the inside of his shirt wet. That's all he knew.

The policeman walked by again on the sidewalk, jabbing the bushes with his nightstick, his partner a few steps behind. Chris cringed back, folding his arms tightly over his chest, holding his breath. The stick jabbed close to his head, and went away. The two policemen walked farther on.

He could follow the bushes along, for a while. Why did everybody have bushes around their houses? It was as if they wanted to help him. They wanted to give him a place to hide.

While he was trying to get home.

The policemen were gone. Chris slid along the base of the bushes and across more backyards. One more street to cross.

≈

Frank stood just outside the nursery door, shaking, listening. Everything was quiet. Lenore had stopped laughing. The TV was off. He breathed deeply, silently, then shoved the door open.

A shaft of light from the hall cut across the crib. Frank slid in along the door. His feet hit toys. They were scattered all over the room.

He took a step toward the crib. It was still. Everything was quiet. He took another step. The light from the hall bathed only the crib, just like (the thought flitted blackly through his mind) the star of Bethlehem. Another step. He looked down at the crib.

Empty.

Naturally.

Lenore. Lenore had been in here, just as she had been in Chris's room. *She* had messed up the toys. She's on the ragged edge, Lenore is. She needs help.

God, if all this would only end, just be over, so he could get her out of here, get her some help, nurse her back. They would all be crazy soon.

He looked down at the crib. He was not checking on her. Not this time. He took the edge of the comforter in his fingers and pulled it back. Slowly he lowered the palm of his other hand. He flattened it on the sheet.

The sheet was warm.

It was not Lenore who had been in that crib.

The door slammed shut behind him.

He stood in the darkness. Terror crept up his legs, up his back, along his neck. He didn't know if he could move. Or should. His leg took a step backward. His breath came in spasms. Then it stopped altogether.

He took another step back, then another. Against the wall. He slid his hand up the wall an inch at a time. The switch. He turned it on.

The room was empty. He was alone.

Lenore was alone too, downstairs.

But he couldn't move. For a minute or two. He stood, seeing nothing, feeling nothing.

"LENORE!" he screamed. Then he could move.

≈≈≈

Chris crawled forward on his hands and knees. He hoped he wouldn't be punished for his pants. It didn't matter. He was almost home. These were bushes he knew, played under when he wanted to be alone, to pretend.

The same police car, back and forth on the street. They couldn't catch him now. They were too late. He was home. He could run to the house.

He sat back on his haunches, gathering his breath for the final sprint.

He scratched the ground with his hands. What was that? Something on the ground. He picked it up, brought it close to his face to see. Some kind of cloth. Torn. Like an old shirt.

He felt around. A pile of the stuff. Rags. Placed neatly, round, hollowed out in the middle. Like a nest.

He would have to find out who'd been messing around in his bushes.

He inched forward to the grass and looked out at the street. He could see the red taillights of the police car as it turned away around the corner.

Now would be good.

But Chris was smart. Already he had learned a lot. Across the street walked two policemen, jabbing their nightsticks into the bushes. They couldn't fool Chris. He would wait until they all were gone.

He wouldn't go for the front door—too easy to be seen. He wouldn't go to the front at all. He'd go around to the back. Not to the back door. It'd be bolted from the inside. But to the cellar door, which had a padlock on it.

He would only have a few seconds, before the police came around again. But that's all he needed.

≋

Frank stumbled down the stairs and lurched through the living room. "Lenore!" She wasn't there, or in the den.

He tore into the kitchen.

Lenore was pressing the hook closed on the cellar door. She spun toward Frank and leaned back heavily against the door.

"Lenore! Lenore!" He grabbed her in his arms. Then he held her away from him. "What were you doing down there?"

She smiled. "In the basement? Oh, just getting . . . a bottle of wine."

"Where is it?"

"What?"

"The wine. You don't have any wine."

"Oh, well," she again leaned against the door, casually, "I couldn't find just what I wanted."

He stared at her, panting, his lips quivering. "No."

"No?"

"What were you doing down there?" He grabbed her and shook her shoulders. "You were down there before too. What were you doing, Lenore?"

She wrenched free, pushed him back, and threw her arms wide against the cellar door. Her eyes widened, she bared her teeth. "Go away! Leave us alone!"

"Who? You and Chris? WHO!" He grabbed her arm, twisted it fiercely.

"You're hurting me."

"WHO, GODDAM IT! WHO!"

Her chest heaved, her breath grated through her throat in a howl. "You know who! YOU KNOW!"

≈≈≈

Chris watched the patrol car cruise by one more time, then lunged out of the bushes and raced across the yard, illuminated for a few feet by the streetlight.

Long enough for Charley to see him disappearing into the shadows to the rear of the house.

He careened his station wagon against the curb and tugged on the inside door handle. It wouldn't move. He yanked on it. It broke off in his hand. He banged on the door with his shoulder. "Chris!" he hollered, the word resounding in his car.

≈≈≈

Chris felt along the outside basement wall for the flowerpot, lifted it, scooped up the key, and probed for the hole in the padlock. He found it, turned the key in it to pop it open, and flipped the lock away. He pulled hard on the big door, lifting it slowly on its hinge. Slithering inside, he let the door close quietly down against his back.

He shivered in the dank cellar, standing on the stone steps for a moment to get his breath. Then he went down the steps and started across the cellar floor toward the sliver of light glowing under the kitchen door at the top of the stairs on the opposite side.

He groped along the familiar passage between the storage stacks, recognizing by touch his sled, his old stroller, the tall pile of old *Life* magazines, the fishing poles, the boxes of Salvation Army clothes.

He stopped.

Eyes. Large eyes looking at him. Across the cellar. "Dad? Mom? Who is it?"

He was afraid, in a way. But not afraid. Something in the eyes made him not afraid. "Who is it? Biscuit?" They were not cat's eyes. Large, round, like his own. "Who is it?"

He worked his way slowly toward the eyes, and heard a low whimpering. "It's okay. I won't hurt you." The whimpering became a steadier cry, still low. "It's okay." He moved closer. It cried and sniffled.

Just a few feet away.

He peered through the darkness. His eyes were growing accustomed to it, his pupils widening like those in the eyes he was looking at. "It's okay."

He could see it now, dimly. He was not afraid. Not at all. Nothing like he had ever seen before. Or even dreamed. But it *was* a baby, and it didn't scare him.

He reached out his hand. The crying stopped. It blinked. Slowly it too raised its hand—its strange, clawed hand—and reached out.

≋

Charley hurled himself against the car door, feeling the tendons tear across his shoulder. The door broke open.

Charley tumbled out, holding his shoulder, and ran for the rear of the house. "Chris—"

≋

Frank backed away from Lenore. His voice quaked. "It's been here. You've seen it. You've been helping it . . ."

They stared wildly at each other.

". . . It's still here, down there. Isn't it? Yes. God, yes!"

He broke for the den, fumbling in his pocket for his keys, ripping them out, tearing his pocket and scattering coins over the floor.

He opened the drawer of the desk and grabbed the .38 and a box of shells.

Lenore ran in behind him, reaching for him, clawing at his back, slashing his shirt. "No! You can't! You can't do it! It's our baby, Frank!"

He swung his elbow, slamming her against the wall.

He tried to push the shells into the chamber. They fell out of the box and rolled on the floor. He managed to load one, two. Enough. He swatted home the cylinder and dashed through the living room and kitchen to the cellar door.

Lenore was right behind him, diving at his hands, tearing them away from the hook. "You *can't!* You *can't!*" She scratched his face and he staggered back. She barred the door with her arms. "HE—COULD—HAVE—KILLED—YOU!" Her voice came in wet, fast gasps. "Yes, it's true. Before, when you were sleeping, he could have killed you. You know it. But he doesn't *want* to kill you. He doesn't *want* to hurt you. You're his *father*—"

He lunged for her, but she slid under his hand, down the door, collapsing on the floor, shivering with sobs.

He sucked for breath, staring at her, fingering the .38.

≋

Charley reached the outside basement door and heaved it open with his one good arm. "Chris?"

He leaned his head down inside the door. "Chris? You down there?"

He heard a soft voice: ". . . Don't be afraid. Nobody will hurt you. My name is Chris . . ."

"Who's down there with you, Chris? Frank? Everything okay?"

". . . Don't be afraid . . ."

The door from the kitchen exploded open, spraying a stream of light.

Chris wheeled toward his father. "Don't—"

"Dive, Chris!" Frank hurtled down the stairs, waving his gun in front of him.

"Dad, don't—"

The thing yowled and leaped from its perch into the shadows.

Frank knocked Chris aside and fired.

The thing screamed and bounded for the outside cellar door.

Frank fired again.

Charley stood silhouetted in the moonlight when the shape hit him. He staggered backward, tearing at it with his hands as it wrapped around his throat. Then he sagged slowly to the ground. The thing slithered away across the grass.

Frank charged up the stone stairs. Charley was lying still on the grass.

Light hit Frank in the face. Two policemen ran up, guns drawn.

"I hit it," Frank said, "I'm sure I hit it at least once."

One of the policemen rolled Charley over, shining his light at the gaping gashes in the throat.

The other policeman ran around the edge of the backyard, flashing his light into the bushes.

Police cars screeched to a halt in front of the house.

"You didn't have to shoot him, Dad." Chris stood behind his kneeling father. His voice was calm. "He wasn't going to hurt anybody."

Frank's body shook with weeping. He bent over his friend. "Look what . . . he did to Charley. Look . . ."

The policeman helped Frank to his feet.

Detective Perkins and several other officers sprinted around the corner of the house.

"We got one dead, lieutenant—there. Name is Charley something."

"Evans," Frank's voice was barely audible, "his name is Charley Evans."

"Davis shoot him?" Detective Perkins snatched Frank's gun hand, then eased the pistol out of it.

"No sir. Throat's been ripped open. Guess it was that thing."

"I hit it, at least once. I shot. I hit it."

Police officers immediately fanned out in a search. Other sirens wailed their approach.

"You see it, Mr. Davis?" Perkins asked.

"Just . . . a blur."

"This your boy here?"

"My name is Chris."

"You see it, Chris?"

"Yes."

"What'd it look like?"

Chris shrugged. "Nobody. Me. Mom. Dad." Suddenly he turned and ran to the back door, where his mother stood holding herself tightly with her arms. "Mom—Mom—"

He threw himself against her. They held each other. "He killed Charley, Mom. He killed poor Charley. He—didn't mean to." Chris wept and they rocked together.

"He killed others too, Chris. He was afraid. He only wants to live. I'm glad you're home, Chris . . ." She took the boy inside and closed the door.

≫≫≫

Detective Perkins examined Frank's .38. "You shouldn't have tried to do this yourself, Davis. Lucky you didn't plug your son."

"I did, I—"

Perkins peered at him.

"I mean, I hit the thing."

Perkins turned to the first two officers. "How'd you guys miss all this?"

"We were cruising, sir, just like we were supposed to. We were by this house at least once every minute. And the foot patrol was on station too. Musta just happened in a few seconds. We never saw that thing go in. I figure it musta been in there for a good while."

"You bastards were responsible," he said softly.

"Yes sir. It's just that, we did what you said, you know, short of going right in the house. And you told us not to do that. And we haven't had any sleep in two days . . ."

"Okay." Perkins chewed his cigar. "Get on the search, goddam it!"

"Lieutenant! Lieutenant!"

Perkins trotted over to the bushes.

"Look here, lieutenant. Blood. Quite a bit. He hit it, all right."

"Here too, lieutenant, over here on this fence. Thing musta climbed over. Losing a lot of blood."

The men traced the trail of blood beyond the bushes and fence into the next yard.

"Here, Lieutenant Perkins." Captain Sanford stood in the gutter and stared down a storm drain. The trail of blood led across the sidewalk to the gutter and over to the drain. The trail stopped there; the blood trickled down through the grate. "I think we got the damn thing now. It's down there."

"Okay, seal off the drains!" Detective Perkins barked fast signals to his men. "Men posted at every opening around here! We'll take the cars to the other end of the feeder! Six men cover this house, four outside and two in! Get Mrs. Davis and the kid outta there, take 'em to the station!"

He started for his car. Frank grabbed his arm. "I'm coming."

"No you ain't."

Frank pushed in front of him. "I have to, lieutenant! I have to be along!"

"You've done enough already. Wounded it. That's plenty. Enough for you."

"No. Not yet!"

Detective Perkins gazed at him, his eyes narrowed. He worked his cigar over to the corner of his mouth. "You may have finished it off already."

"Maybe not. I've gotta come! I've gotta be there when you find it."

Detective Perkins looked off into the distance, then back at Frank. "So you gotta do it yourself."

"It's mine. My problem. Try to understand. Be more than a cop. Understand what I'm saying. You may need me. Try to understand . . ."

"I understand, Mr. Davis. It may not always look like it, but that's my job. Between us, I figured all along that this thing might be heading here—might be trying to get to its mother, in fact. In a way I was *using* you. But I thought we'd spot it first, was sure of it. Otherwise I never would have tried it. We blew it, that's all. So you ended up having to take some pot-shots. Now, I know what you're saying. But I don't even hear it. I never heard it. You just get in my car, on your own. Don't ask questions, don't answer none."

"Thanks, lieutenant." Frank closed his eyes. "I thank you for—"

"Shut up. And here, take this." He handed Frank back his .38. "It's yours. Put it away. Don't use it. We'll get this thing. No sense in us both being out of a job."

≋

Professor Eckstein stared down at the report Dr. Norten had written, several pages, single-spaced, its front cover marked, "Absolutely Secret and Confidential: Nobody Open."

"It's all there, professor." Dr. Norten beamed.

Eckstein scanned the pages, flipping them over one after the other. "I see . . ."

"Yes! I processed the final lab reports on Mrs. Davis myself. Even *she* doesn't know."

"And it's just like I—we had theorized."

"To the penny!"

"This is terribly important, doctor—ominous. I suppose now we should release it to—"

"No no NO!" Norten grabbed the document and hugged it to his chest. "That is, not yet. We must, of course, await the final autopsy reports on the thing itself."

"But meanwhile shouldn't we alert—"

"We can't breathe a word, professor. Just a little

longer. If we released this now—you know how the scientific community is, they'd just scoff at us for an incomplete study. Call us amateurs. Scaremongers. They wouldn't believe us. Listen to me: we do this right, it's the Nobel Prize for us. You hear that? The *Nobel!* Rich! Famous!"

"I'm not so sure I care about being—"

"And above all, professional!" Dr. Norten said, jabbing an index finger in the air. "Professionalism is good timing. We'll be professional by sitting on this for a while, until the world is ready for it."

≈

Buck Clayton stared out over the lights of Beverly Hills. It had been a very bad day.

Today old man Marcus canceled the account.

Not for the reason that his toy business had turned sour overnight—which it had. Nobody would touch a Marcus toy. It was those pictures that did that. Goddam pictures on KBOP-TV. Taken right in the school. Pictures of the toys that vampire kid had been messing with. Identified as Marcus toys.

How in hell'd the TV people find out about that? How in hell'd they get in there to photograph them? Those pictures knocked the bottom right out of the Marcus toy business.

But that wasn't why old man Marcus pulled out.

He pulled out, he said, because Frank Davis was no longer on the account. If Davis had been around to manage things, the old man said, those pictures never would have happened. So Buck Clayton stared out the huge window at the lights and wondered what he'd done to get himself in such a pickle.

There were a million Frank Davises.

Why in hell'd *his* Frank Davis have to go and father a freak kid?

≈

They stood on the spillway outside the end of an enormous pipe, one of those that form the vast subterranean storm-drain tunnel system that underlies Los Angeles. A police car sat with its nose in the pipe, and still there was room for men to pass in on either side. After a heavy rain, a torrent of water would flush out of this pipe and flood the spillway. Tonight it was nearly dry.

The portable floodlights arrayed by police caused Frank to squint as he approached the tunnel entrance with Detective Perkins.

Frank peered into the blackness within the tunnel of huge pipe.

"No guarantee we'll find it in there quick," said Perkins. "We got men coming in from other directions. But the drains branch off every which way. It won't get out. But it may take us a while. We ain't gonna be comfortable in there. Sure you want to come along?"

Frank nodded.

"All right. Now, we'll take a car in there a ways, far as it can go, so we'll have lights from that for a while. Then all we got's our flashlights. Don't get lost."

Frank shook his head.

"Let's go."

The band of hunters dressed in blue police uniforms marched into the tunnel, followed by the car, which spread its light beams over them and beyond.

The floodlit entrance quickly vanished as they moved around a bend. It was cold and dank. Water gurgled over their shoes. Sounds of their walking and breathing echoed along the pipe.

Another group of men appeared, coming toward them from a branch tunnel to the left. "Clear, lieutenant, all the way out this one."

The band took the branch to the right, leaving the patrol car and its lights behind. Their flashlights flickered off the water and the dark stone walls.

More branches. Detective Perkins split the men into smaller squads and sent them off into each new branch they passed. The sounds of their splashing through the water, their giving and answering commands, their grunting, wheezing, coughing, and panting bounced off the damp stone and echoed down the tunnels. It was impossible to tell where each sound was coming from.

≋

They had been in the tunnel for more than an hour, Frank guessed. They had doubled back through countless branches, meeting men emerging from some, sending other men off in new ones. Detective Perkins seemed to know just where they were. To Frank it was a total mystery. He had no sense of direction at all. For all he knew, they could be under Pasadena by now.

He began to lag behind. He stopped and sagged against the wall, watching the others go on, their lights waving around ahead of them.

The past days of exhaustion gripped him, weighted him down. He could barely keep his eyes open. And he was cold. Chilled beyond all recollection of warmth. He pulled his jacket tight across his chest and buried his chin in the collar.

His light was dimming, and he snapped it off to save the batteries.

He slumped against the wall in the dark, the unreasonable cold numbing him. Nothing seemed important except to get warm and to sleep. He closed his eyes, but that didn't help. When he opened them, it was as if he could suddenly see what he only heard.

Silence.

The police were gone. He was alone in the tunnel.

He turned on his flashlight and moved forward, along the route where he had seen the police advancing. His feet were numb, down in the rivulet of water.

He should call out. But the notion of that sound erupting in echoes around him chilled him more.

He slogged along staring ahead into the gloom beyond the dimming beam of his flashlight. Passing black holes that would be entrances to other branches of the maze, he stayed in the main channel. Eventually he would find the police officers, if he kept on in this direction. But he didn't. He gazed blankly at the entrance to yet another pipe and decided to go in that way for a while.

He hadn't gone far when he heard the sound. A low, weak, human moan.

Where?

The sound seemed to come from everywhere. Each way he turned, the frail sound bounced off the stone. But since he hadn't heard it before, it must be ahead.

He stuck his hand into his jacket pocket and felt the icy metal of his .38. He took it out. He should have it ready.

He stepped up the pace on his aching legs, his revolver clacking against the stone wall as he steadied himself with that hand and held his light with the other. The sound was a bit louder now, a moan of sickness or sadness or pain. A pleading baby's haunting whine.

≈≈≈

"Must not be in here, lieutenant. I think we been everywhere."

"It's here. Where's Davis?"

"Davis? He was right behind us."

"Well, he ain't now. Find a manhole, go topside, use your radio, find out if Davis surfaced anywhere."

"Yes sir."

"Okay, all you men. Let's double back. Davis is probably back there somewhere."

The men turned and began retracing the tunnel.

"You think he went out, lieutenant?" a patrolman asked.

"Nope."

"He shoulda stuck with us. He don't know his way around in here."

"Any *other* news for me, patrolman?"

"No sir. One good thing . . ."

"What's that?"

"At least he's got his .38 with him. Sorry, but I saw you give it back to him."

"You think I'm a fool? It ain't loaded. And he don't have no shells on him—I know 'cause I patted him down while you guys were looking around the yard."

"You didn't want him armed?"

"Course not. I value both my job and my life. He ain't trained with that. He felt better with it on him, that's all. Take a left up here, you four men," he called behind him. "We're only about a quarter-mile from where we left the car."

"What if we don't find him, lieutenant?"

"What if! What if! Goddam it, patrolman, will you watch where you're going and quit stepping on my feet!"

A man ran toward them. "Davis didn't come out! Nobody's seen him!"

"Okay. I'm taking two men down this way here to the right. Rest of you go on ahead. When you get out, mobilize some cars upstairs. This is the last section. At least we'll find Davis and get him the hell out of here. If we don't find the other thing we're after, get everybody right back down in here, in this section. We'll start all over. GO!"

The rest of the men scampered on ahead. Perkins

and his two officers veered off to the right, into a branch he wasn't entirely sure they had searched before.

〰

Frank's footsteps echoed in the tunnel as he moved slowly toward the continuous whimpering sound. He held his flashlight and his gun out in front of him. His eyes burned from his incessant peering into the bleak mist.

He passed another branch tunnel and continued. The sound faded. He backtracked to the opening.

It had to be in there.

He went in. The sound was closer, more distinct. He could hear the soft hiccuping now between sobs.

It was in front of him. He shined his light straight ahead. The tunnel faded into empty blackness. But it was right in front of him. Slowly he lowered his light, toward the floor.

There, on a slab of stone slightly elevated above the water, it sat.

A small, shivering thing of pale, smooth, almost translucent skin. Veins pulsed visibly in the temples of the large, bulbous head which seemed to rest directly on its narrow shoulders. Its legs and clawed feet were folded in front of its belly, which undulated with its breathing. Its short, thin arms and clawed fingers waggled spasmodically in front of its chest.

It sat there just like a baby.

It cried softly and sniffled as it looked at him with its huge, round, black eyes.

Frank extended his arm and raised the gun evenly until he could sight down the barrel at a spot between its eyes.

It made no move, just whimpered and looked at him, its prominent pointed teeth appearing now and then as it curled its lips in sobs. Tears from the black eyes rolled down its face and body. The eyes blinked, and Frank blinked back.

He saw the blood. He lowered the gun. Blood oozed down under one arm, down the side, onto the stone. It formed a pool amid the small pile of rags on which the thing sat.

It moaned more loudly and blinked and reached one clawed hand around to feel where the blood was coursing down its side.

"Sssh." Frank dropped the gun, it clattered on the stone. "I know it hurts, but it's going to be all right."

It closed its eyes, weeping silently.

Frank knelt in front of it and slid forward on his knees. "I hurt you. I'm sorry. I was scared, like you were. But don't cry. Don't cry any more. They'll hear you. They'll come and . . . You know I won't hurt you again."

It opened its eyes and they looked at each other, blinking. It shivered.

"I won't hurt you again."

"Davis!"

He stiffened.

"Davis! You in there? Wherever you are, stay there! We'll find you!"

The thing began to moan.

"No, no, it's okay. Don't cry any more. I'll take care of you. You're cold."

He peeled off his jacket, stood up, and stepped forward, holding the jacket carefully in front of him. "I'll take care of you. This will make you warm. Don't cry. This will make you warm." Gently he lowered the jacket over it, wrapped it snugly, and picked it up, cradling it in his arms.

It nestled against him, fully enclosed by the jacket, trembling.

Frank began walking in the darkness.

"Davis! We'll find you!"

Frank's tears tumbled onto the jacket in his arms.

He felt the warm moisture of the blood soaking through on his hands. "I'll take care of you."

"Davis! If you can hear me, give a holler! This is Perkins! Stay where you are!"

The voice was closer now.

Frank ran, stumbling, splashing through the tunnel.

"Davis! Hold it! Stop!"

They were behind him. Their lights glistened along the wall over his shoulders. He ran, clutching the shivering bundle in his arms.

Another light, up ahead, coming from the top of the tunnel. An opening. Metal rungs going up the side.

His eyes blurred with tears, his heart raged hot in his chest, his lungs fought for room to breathe. He stumbled, lurched, fell to his knees, holding the bundle tight. A wail of pain came from inside the jacket.

He struggled to his feet, steadying himself against the side of the tunnel with his shoulder. "I fell. I'm sorry. I have you now. Nobody will hurt you."

He ran.

The metal rungs. He held the bundle under his left arm and reached for them with his right.

"Davis! You can't get away, Davis! There's no place for you to go! Let us help you!"

He missed the rungs, slipped and fell to his knees again. He reached, stretched, grabbed for the lowest rung, got his fingers around it, clamped them on it, and pulled himself erect.

"Hold it, Davis!"

Frank turned.

Detective Perkins stood a few yards away. He held up his hand. There was no gun in it.

"No."

"I'm not gonna do anything to you, or to your friend there."

"No."

"Give it up, Davis. Nowhere to go. I'm the best help you got, right now."

The other policemen behind Perkins edged forward. They had guns in their hands.

"No."

Perkins held out his arms, keeping the other officers behind him. "Between us, Davis. We can keep it between us. It's over."

"No." Frank pulled himself partway up the ladder.

A policeman lunged forward. Perkins caught him by the collar and hauled him back.

Frank stared down at them. He was near the exit hole now. Dim light shone over his head. The bundle shivered under his left arm. Frank held it tightly.

He stared at Detective Perkins. Perkins stood still, looking up at him. Slowly, casually, he reached into his jacket pocket and took out a cigar. He licked it and put it into his mouth. He chewed on it. Otherwise he didn't move. He looked at Frank without blinking.

"There's a whole world out there, Davis," he said softly. "And it ain't always friendly."

Frank turned and looked up, through the hole. He tightened his grip on the rung above him.

Then suddenly he leaped up and clambered out.

He was blinded. Headlights from a dozen cars flashed on in his face. He closed his eyes and stood cradling his bundle in both arms.

The thing wrapped in his jacket stirred, pulling at the fabric, nails scratching through on Frank's arms. "I'll take care of you. Nobody will hurt you."

It moaned, then the moan deepened, became hoarse, became a growl.

"Nobody will hurt you!"

"DROP IT, DAVIS!"

He opened his eyes, narrowing them to see through the blinding light.

"THIS IS CAPTAIN SANFORD OF THE STATE POLICE!" The voice came over a bullhorn. "YOU'RE SURROUNDED BY ARMED MEN! DROP IT!"

"I won't let anybody hurt you."

It growled and squirmed. Frank held it tight.

Detective Perkins and his men climbed out of the manhole and stood a few yards behind Frank.

He could see the Troopers in front of him now, inching forward, their rifles trained on him.

"I'll take care of you."

"DROP IT, DAVIS!"

Then he could see Captain Sanford, bearing the bullhorn in one hand and his Magnum in the other, advancing slowly ahead of the others.

"No."

He could see Lenore too, standing near one of the cars. The lights sparkled on her face, shimmered in her tears.

Sanford dropped the bullhorn on the ground and came closer. "Lieutenant, better get your men out of my line of fire. And Troopers, everybody, off to one side. This guy's armed."

The Troopers scurried around to form an arc to Captain Sanford's right. Detective Perkins and his men stayed right where they were, directly behind Frank.

Sanford was just a few feet away now. He stopped. "Drop it, Davis. Drop it and step away. I'm gonna blast it right here and now."

Frank looked at him. "You don't need to," he called softly. "It's hurt. It can't do anything."

"Don't be a sap, Davis. We gotta get rid of it."

"Lock it up, but let it live. Please let it live."

"Whether you're holding it or not, in five seconds I'm putting a bullet through it. One. Two——"

Suddenly the growl from within the jacket became a shriek. It writhed viciously and tore through. It sprang from Frank's arms, leaping through the air at Captain Sanford. He got off one shot from his Magnum before the thing hit his throat.

He staggered backward and fell, grasping futilely at the demon whose claws and teeth sank deep into his neck.

In the same seconds, Detective Perkins dove, landing on his belly beside them. He jammed the nose of his pistol against the side of the snarling, clawing form and squeezed off four quick shots.

For a few moments, all was still.

Then men raced forward to pour over the scene, stooping down at the bodies of the captain and the creature crumpled beside him.

Frank stumbled over to Lenore and fell against her, wrapped his arms around her, supported by her, sobbing onto her shoulder as she sobbed into his chest. "It's over. Darling, it's—over. It *was* ours. I'm sorry—"

≋

Detective Perkins helped them into the backseat and he slid into the front beside the driver.

"Where to, sir?"

"Nowhere. Sit."

Frank and Lenore leaned together in the back, their hands and arms intertwined, their wet eyes closed.

Perkins stared out his open window at the turmoil of policemen, ambulance attendants, and various officials who milled around, shouting and cursing. He rolled up the window.

The radiophone buzzed. The driver picked up the receiver. "For you, lieutenant."

Detective Perkins took the receiver, held it against the seat for a moment, then put it to his ear. "Yeah? . . . I see. Yeah." He worked the cigar around in his mouth. "I understand. Right."

He put the receiver back in its cradle and turned to look at Frank and Lenore. Slowly he took the cigar out of his mouth. "Another one has been born in Seattle."

They gazed dumbly at him.

He turned away and stared out the window. They all stared out.

Dawn's light filtered through the smog over Los Angeles. It was the beginning of a bright new day.